My Valiant Princess

A Small-Town Shifter Romance

Shelley Munro

Munro Press

DEDICATION

For Paul, my partner in crime and fellow adventurer.

INTRODUCTION

PRINCESS ALLEGRA WOLFEHART WILL stop at nothing to save her people from the corruption in her kingdom. But when an attempt is made on her life, she realizes threats lurk around every corner.

Werewolf Dylan Stewart is living a peaceful life in New Zealand until his sister's best friend, Princess Allegra, arrives to visit. With her beauty and determination, she turns his world upside down. However, danger follows Allegra to Middlemarch and threatens their budding romance.

Will their love withstand the challenges, or will Allegra's enemies snuff it out before their relationship has the chance to bloom?

Get ready for a thrilling caper in the kingdom of Val-des-Loups and Middlemarch, New Zealand. Don't miss this heart-pumping adventure of love, danger, and werewolves.

1

Allegra Wolfehart's footsteps echoed loudly as she stormed down the spiral staircase hidden deep within the walls of Chateau-Loup. The sheer ridiculousness of the council members' conversation astounded her. No! It left her pissed and irate.

The utter rubbish.

The lies.

This pack of wolves, meant to cooperate for their species' welfare, had dismissed her ideas to prevent deforestation. Despite the kingdom's ample resources, they justified their actions by citing the enormous financial gain. They didn't need more money. Hadn't they heard of budgets?

Sophia, Gabriel, and Emilio had ignored her pleas for aid for the struggling werewolves in the west, disregarded her proposals, and acted as if her voice didn't matter. She was the princess of Val-des-Loups and the sole remaining royal, but they'd treated her like an infant. The response from Maria, Andreas, and Maximillian had been as damning.

Silence.

Was the entire council against her? She didn't know, but the idea of innocent wolves suffering made her skin crawl and fire rage in her blood.

As she emerged from the staircase, a pair of chateau security guards, older wolves who'd known her as a young pup, greeted her. She tried to muster a smile, but agitation from her wolf rippled through her mind in smoky gray waves.

"Is everything okay, Princess Allegra?" one of them asked.

Damn. Given their scrutiny, her eyes were glowing with werewolf gold intensity instead of her normal blue. She exhaled deeply, trying to rein in her inner wolf.

"Yes, thank you." Allegra fought to keep her voice steady. "I have a headache after the meeting. Some fresh air should do the trick."

The guards stepped aside with deference, their

boots creating a sharp echo as they tapped against the marble tiles. The fabric of their uniforms swished and rustled. Allegra marched through the chateau's resplendent halls, her heavy footsteps reverberating off the walls. She ignored the servants' curious stares, her focus on the injustice of the council's decision.

What was her next move?

She gritted her teeth, determination coursing through her veins because she refused to let this pass. The logging must end. Their forests had dwindled at an alarming rate while the council didn't seem to understand that werewolves needed nature to thrive. What would her parents have done? Her brother?

A lump formed in her throat as she tried to recall the sharp details of their faces. An assassin had snatched her family from her, and their deaths had left a yawning hole in her heart.

Her parents—the king and queen of Val-des-Loups—had been influential leaders, and she prayed she'd live up to their legacy. She wondered if they'd be proud of her now as she struggled to gain the council's support. The grief was so tangible, a physical presence, and her vision blurred as she slipped through a side door and exited the chateau. *Princesses controlled their emotions.* She swiped her hand over her face and inhaled the fresh, spicy scent of the breeze.

Outside, the warm hues of a late afternoon cast a golden glow over the chateau's manicured gardens. The tinkling of water falling from a statue's urn into the pond below didn't provide the usual tranquility. A lonely hawk's cry echoed from the trees beyond the chateau walls, piercing the stillness.

Another wave of misery flooded her, and Allegra barely registered the beauty around her as she marched across the courtyard toward the chateau's boundary fence. With a backward glance, she slipped through a gate and beelined for the edge of the royal forest. When she reached the trees, she paused and listened to the rustling leaves. The cool air hit her face as she inhaled, trying to calm her mental state. But it was no use. The helpless fury that boiled within her refused to budge.

Allegra scanned her surroundings again, and once she confirmed she was alone, she yanked off her sneakers. Next came her jeans and tailored shirt—her nod to the council's stuffy need for formal apparel, then her underwear. With ease of practice, she folded her clothing and tucked it and her shoes in a dry spot, out of sight of a casual observer.

Yet another tear streamed down her face, and she wiped it away with an impatient brush. Crying solved nothing. Neither would nursing her hurt sensibilities. She required concrete ideas and a way to exert her authority over the council. Although only twenty-three, she was far from stupid. Finishing school had taught her well, and with her bookkeeping skills, she could tell something was off with the royal accounts.

Allegra drew in a deep breath, rich in forest greenery, and let it drift back out. She repeated this, exhaling slowly as her brother had taught her to combat her anxiety about public appearances. His advice worked then, and it did now. More centered, she called up her wolf.

When her transformation began, she convulsed with the usual pain and didn't fight the natural progression. Bones cracked and rearranged themselves. Her skin itched and burned as hair sprouted from every pore. Primal power and energy surged through her veins, a sense of triumph and rightness as she fell to all fours. The world around her shifted, colors and sounds becoming sharper and more vibrant. Exhilaration and freedom washed over her as she broke into a run, her feet thudding against the leaf-strewn dirt path. Allegra embraced nature and fled deeper into the dense pine and spruce forest.

But the sense of peace she craved didn't come, her mind still racing with anger and frustration. How could the council members act so heartlessly? Didn't they see the suffering of their kind? Allegra had to do something, but what? She couldn't sit idly by and watch as her people grew weaker and drifted from traditional pack ties or worse turned to crime.

She pushed herself harder and farther than she ever had before. The wind whipped through her fur, and the rustle of tiny woodland creatures scurrying to safety reached her ears. She needed to find a solution, but her mind was a blank screen.

On and on she ran, the trees ending without warning. Allegra jerked to a halt, stumbling into the clearing. It was not the natural forest beauty that caught her attention. Enormous machinery had torn up this ground, leaving massive scars on the earth. Someone had felled the majestic trees that had stood here for hundreds of years. The scent of sawdust led her to a pile of logs stacked in a neat heap.

This was not the work of nature.

It was intentional.

The council?

She'd bet the contents of her bank account on this assumption.

Allegra's heart sank at this additional proof of the council's corruption. Their greed extended even into the sanctity of the old forest.

She stared at the desecration, a fierce growl rumbling through her chest. The birds ceased singing, emphasizing the rustle of leaves in the gentle breeze.

Allegra's head snapped up, a warning prickling her neck. The fur down her back stood on end. She listened intently while she surveyed the vicinity, searching for the source while every sense screamed of imminent danger.

A sharp crack pierced the hush of the forest, and she flinched as a piece of bark flew off the tree trunk next to her. The muffled *phut* made her jump. Instantly, she crouched, making herself small, her light brown fur blending with the undergrowth.

Gun.

Her muscles trembled, her entire body tensing. A second shot hit a nearby tree. Allegra didn't hesitate.

Someone was shooting at her. It was time to beat a hasty retreat.

Back at the chateau, Allegra skipped taking a shower. On top of discovering corruption within the council, the alarm bells were deafening. Someone had shot at her.

She grabbed a backpack from her wardrobe and began to pack. She added two changes of clothes, toiletries, a few personal items, her phone, passport, and wallet. At the last moment, she threw in the box with the lucky runes her older brother had given her as a secret present. Her throat tightened at the thought of her brother. He'd promised to explain the origins of the runes when she was older. That wouldn't happen now.

During her furious run from the forest back to the chateau, she'd reached a conclusion. Her people would suffer if she died, so she needed to step away briefly and make plans.

Allegra snatched up her daypack and slung it over one shoulder. She could catch a late flight to Rome and, from there, a flight to Sydney despite the late hour. If anyone tried to track her, it would take them time. She'd further muddy her trail if she paid for the fare with her private funds instead of her official credit card. At least, she hoped that would happen. She hated to take trouble with her but couldn't think of another location the council wouldn't quickly discover.

Her friend had lived in Scotland but had moved to Middlemarch in New Zealand last year. Esther's blunt nature allowed her to point out Allegra's mistakes and clarify whether Allegra imagined skullduggery where there was none.

She hurried down the curving marble staircase from the second floor to the main entrance, her right hand tracing the ornate banister and the intricate designs of wolves and other mythical creatures. She needed to act normally, despite the urge for a furtive exit.

The scent of freshly cut flowers wafted to her, the cream blooms arranged in crystal vases placed strategically around the main foyer. The rays of the setting sun pierced the stained-glass windows, casting a rainbow of colors across the marble surfaces.

As she neared the ground floor, the faint murmur of voices told her dinner preparations were underway.

The formal dining room meals were strained because of her push-back at meetings. Her mouth twisted. These dinners were a recent development, as were the council members moving into the chateau and treating it like their home.

"Ah, Allegra. Just in time for drinks." Gabriel appeared at the doorway of a formal lounge. He wore a dark suit, his gray tie arranged with precision. It contrasted nicely with his mane of silver hair.

Maria appeared beside Gabriel, dressed in a form-fitting red dress. Her dark brows arched in puzzlement. "Allegra, where are you going? Dinner is almost ready. We have roast beef."

"I told the housekeeper earlier. I've made plans to meet Janet for dinner," Allegra said.

"Is everything okay?" Gabriel asked, narrowing his eyes. His black brows highlighted the intensity of his gaze.

Allegra's heart raced, and her hand tightened on her bag. Losing her temper again would achieve nothing. "Yes, everything's fine," she lied, praying they wouldn't press her further.

"Please inform one of us in future," Maria said, her voice strident. "Sometimes, we have guests who are important to the kingdom. They like to meet the family."

What was she? A performing pony?

"Of course." Allegra breathed a sigh of relief when they waved her off, and she hustled outside to the garage, where she kept her car. Every step felt like it took too long, every breath too shallow. She had to retreat before someone else tried to stop her.

"Good evening, Princess Allegra," a man said.

Allegra jumped, her heart leaping halfway up her throat. She pressed her hand to her chest, the *thud-thud-thud* hard against her fingers as she whirled to face him.

"Sorry, I didn't mean to startle you." His expression held contrition.

"No apology necessary. My thoughts were elsewhere."

The man nodded respectfully. "Were you taking out the car?"

"Yes." Allegra's pulse raced, and she was confident he would hear and wonder at her anxiety, but thankfully, he didn't comment.

"I'll back it out for you," he said, polite and straightforward.

Five minutes later, she was on her way. Allegra clenched the wheel as she drove along the winding chateau road and constantly checked her mirror. But no one followed her.

Once she reached town, she pulled into a shopping mall and quickly found a store to purchase clothes to change her appearance. Casual clothes—jeans, a white T-shirt, and a nondescript black jacket. She donned them and packed the more formal clothes into her daypack.

After arranging her hair into a tight knot and placing a hat on her head, she also slipped on dark glasses. Hopefully, enough to avoid recognition.

Allegra left her car in the shopping mall car park and walked several blocks before hailing a cab. She passed dozens of people, werewolves and humans, and no one paid her attention. Allegra jumped at every sound during the cab ride and the wait in line to purchase airline tickets.

By the time she'd gone through security, she was noticeably jittery. *Calm.* Otherwise, the officials would notice and remember her passing through immigration.

When she finally stepped onto the aircraft and

found her seat, she released a deep sigh of relief. She was safe. With a shaky hand, she fastened her seatbelt, exhaustion catching up with her. The plane took off, and Allegra's tense muscles relaxed, her eyes closing. The past few days' events had taken their toll, and the road ahead would be difficult. But for now, she allowed herself a moment of respite, grateful for the plane's temporary safety and the engines' comforting hum.

2

DUNEDIN AIRPORT HEAVED WITH passenger arrivals. Allegra dodged a young blond boy still learning to drive his wheely suitcase and stepped through a door leading to the public area. Loud chatter battered her ears, and welcoming cries echoed in the enormous terminal. A crowd of men, women, and children waited for their loved ones. Some held aloft signs while others clutched flowers and balloons, gazes full of excited expectation. She checked each face, searching for Esther.

For a moment, fear swamped her, but no, her friend had promised to meet her during their hurried phone call from Sydney. Sensing the weight of a stare, she turned to the right and spotted Esther waving and calling her name. Allegra broke into a huge grin and ran. Their arms came around each other, and they hugged tightly.

"It's so good to see you." Allegra's throat thickened with emotion.

Esther pulled back an arm's length and offered a warm smile, her long chestnut hair cascading down her back in loose waves. "It's been too long. I was so excited to hear from you, and when you told me you were coming to visit, I was beside myself."

Lush lashes framed her bright hazel eyes, and her high cheekbones and pointed chin gave her an elegant appearance. Allegra noticed a man hovering behind her friend. A friend or someone more important to Esther? He was tall and muscular, with broad shoulders and chiseled features. He wore jeans and a navy-blue T-shirt that got a workout from his pectoral muscles and biceps. Her gaze roved onward to inspect his short, tousled brown hair and strong jawline covered in a hint of stubble. Rugged and alluring. *Nice.*

The man coughed. *Busted!* Allegra started, heat crawling into her cheeks as she met intense hazel eyes. Her breath hissed out because that stare of his pierced right through her.

Esther chortled, and Allegra blushed, wanting to hide from the embarrassment.

"Allegra, this is my brother, Dylan Stewart."

"Nice to meet you, Allegra," Dylan said, his voice deep and smooth. Amusement crept into his tone. "Esther has told me a lot about you."

A shiver ran down Allegra's spine. Esther hadn't mentioned her brother was a hunk. She nodded in response, suddenly shy and unsure of herself. Good grief. She'd studied him like a plate of her favorite hazelnut gelato.

"How was your flight?" Esther asked, breaking Allegra's reverie.

"Long." Allegra focused on the conversation instead of dwelling on her mortification. "I'm exhausted."

"Well, I'm thrilled you're here. How long are you staying? You'll love Middlemarch. Moving here with our pack was the best decision Dylan and I have ever made." Esther chattered non-stop, not giving Allegra a chance to reply. "What have you been up to? I thought you were too busy doing princess things to fit in a visit to a mere commoner."

"*Pffff.*" Allegra hated to discuss her current

dilemma now. She wanted one evening to decompress without the weight of her kingdom bearing down on her shoulders. "I'm sure the kingdom will get along fine without me—at least in the short term. I'm here for five days." Any longer, and she risked the council blocking her return. They were so full of themselves that they'd consider a coup.

Dylan took possession of her daypack, his dark brows arching when she informed him she was traveling light and didn't have a suitcase.

"Tell me more about Middlemarch," Allegra said as they left the airport.

Esther's face lit up as she prattled. "We live a short drive from the town. Unlike your kingdom's principal town, Middlemarch is tiny, but we have a pub, a superette, a lovely cafe, a police station, and a motor vehicle repair place. It's mainly a farming community, but our pack has a woodworking business. We're close to Dunedin if we want to shop for clothes or bigger ticket items."

"But you're in the country and can shift and run?" Allegra asked.

"We have to watch for humans, but there's a large shifter community," Dylan said. "We go on evening runs and have social functions together."

"Allegra, I'm sorry about your parents and brother. It must've been difficult taking over without the necessary training," Esther said, her tone full of compassion. "This is a lousy way to fulfill your wish for more than charity work."

Allegra swallowed hard. "It's a challenge, that's for sure."

She met Dylan's gaze in the rear-vision mirror and glanced away. His musky, masculine scent called her, and she silently railed at her instant attraction. She had no time for romance. When she finally searched for a partner, she needed a man willing to stand at her side and act as a consort, a man to play her backup. Her instincts screamed that Dylan was a take-charge wolf, not one to remain in the background.

She tried to concentrate on Esther's bright chitchat but sneaked glances at Dylan instead. Finally, she forced herself to study the scenery. It differed from the lush pine-clad mountains of Val-des-Loups. The ground here was open, with rolling green hills and flat fields. When they neared Middlemarch, she spotted more hills of tussock grass and gray boulders stacked one atop the other. The rocks reminded her of a child's building blocks.

Dylan veered onto a gravel side road and traveled about two kilometers before turning into a driveway.

"Home, sweet home," Esther said.

The house was a single-level weatherboard home. The walls were dull green and needed a fresh coat of paint, and the gardens desperately needed tending, with tall grasses and weeds obscuring their beauty.

"We're renovating as time and our budget allows." Esther gestured at the house. "Dylan and I bought it together. You should've seen it when we first arrived."

"It must be lovely owning your home and planning what part you'll redo next." Allegra climbed from the car. "The chateau is beautiful, but history is important, and we can't make changes. Tradition plays a big part in my world."

Dylan grabbed her bag from the trunk and insisted on carrying it inside. Allegra followed Esther and her brother, and to her dismay, her gaze wandered to Dylan's backside. Everything about him drew her, but duty was more important than romance.

DYLAN HAD HEARD MUCH about Princess Allegra

Wolfehart but had never met her, mainly because he'd had work and pack duties when Allegra had visited Esther in Scotland. The woman was gorgeous, with her black hair, blue eyes, and quiet manner. She was tired from her flight, yet a fluid grace to her movements spoke of comfort with her body.

He'd expected someone snobby who might look down on him and had mentioned it to Esther. His sister had laughed and told him that Allegra was most unprincesslike and would never use her position to belittle others. She'd told him Allegra hadn't expected to rule, and Dylan admired her sacrifices in taking up the responsibility. Her entire life would've changed, and she'd have had to deal with the running of the kingdom while mourning her parents' and brother's death.

Which begged the question—why was she here now?

He found himself curious about this princess werewolf.

Dylan decided to give Allegra time alone with his sister. He'd promised Rory he'd help deliver a dressing table to a client in Queenstown later this afternoon. He might as well leave now.

Dylan carried the daypack to his sister's room. Esther had told him she and Allegra had shared at school, and it would be lovely to relive old times. He returned to the kitchen and paused in the doorway just in time to hear his sister.

"All right, Allegra. It's lovely to see you, and you're welcome here anytime, but something is happening. You're the crown princess with an entire country to run. Why are you here?"

Allegra lifted her chin, sending Esther an imperious stare that warned her to back off.

Esther made a scoffing sound. "Sit, I'll make a pot of tea, and we'll talk."

"I'm here on holiday," Allegra lied, her voice even and tone so controlled Dylan could taste the deceit.

"Allegra." Esther plonked a plate of sultana scones on the table before her. "You can't lie. Tell me everything now, so we can enjoy the rest of your holiday before you return."

"Something's going on with the council," Allegra finally said.

Dylan watched the princess closely. She sat across from Esther, her hands tightly clasped in her lap as she recounted the events that had led her to flee to

Middlemarch.

"I haven't a clue what to do." Allegra's voice trembled so much that Dylan had the urge to scoop her into his lap to offer comfort. He restrained himself and continued to eavesdrop, feeling not the slightest bit of shame.

Allegra continued, "Someone fired at me when I was in wolf form, and I don't feel secure at the chateau any longer."

Esther's eyes widened. "Who would do something like that? Are you sure it wasn't hunters? Humans can't tell the difference between wolves and werewolves."

"I don't know, but it seems strange after someone assassinated my parents and brother. But that's not all," Allegra continued. "The council's decisions are worrying me. Despite my order, they've sold off logging rights to our forest. Our people need the wilderness to thrive in this modern world."

Esther leaned forward, and Dylan had no difficulty reading the concern on her face. "What are you going to do?"

"I must return, but I need time to think and devise a plan. I couldn't do that at the chateau," Allegra said, her anxiety palpable in the twist of her fingers. She paused, her hands trembling. "I'm worried, Esther. What if I fail my people? What if I can't figure out how to fix everything?"

Esther took Allegra's hand, giving it a comforting squeeze. "You won't buckle. You're strong, smart, and have the support of those who love you. We'll figure this out together."

As the conversation ended, Dylan straightened and entered the kitchen. His eyes fixed on Allegra.

"Hey there." He offered Allegra a small smile. "Is everything okay?"

Allegra looked up, startled. "Dylan!"

Esther chuckled. "He's always lurking somewhere. Don't mind him."

Dylan rolled his eyes but grinned. "So, what's going on? Someone shot at you? That's troubling."

Allegra nodded, her eyes darkening with worry. "Yeah, it was scary. I needed to escape from the chateau to clear my head."

"I don't blame you," Dylan said, aiming for sympathetic. "It sounds like you're going through a lot right now."

Allegra picked up her teacup and took a sip. "I'm

not sure what to do next. Face the council, yes, but I need to figure out a workable plan, especially since I'm one person against six. I don't know how deep the rot goes in Val-des-Loups."

Esther reached for a scone and nudged the plate toward Allegra in a silent demand to eat. "It's good you're taking time out. Dylan and I will help, and the Feline Council might assist. Saber Mitchell has contacts everywhere." She grinned, displaying sharp white teeth. "You're not the only royalty in Middlemarch, you know."

Dylan studied Allegra with newfound respect and took a seat. The woman was gutsy and determined, judging by the set of her jaw. "You require courage to face a situation like this head-on."

Allegra blushed, a charming swathe of color highlighting her cheeks. "Thanks. I hope I'm doing the right thing. I worry the council will overstep more now that I've disappeared."

"What if they think someone kidnapped you?" Esther set down her tea with a sharp clunk. Her expression grim, she picked up her phone and started tapping keys.

"And what if this council decides your

disappearance gives them the perfect opportunity to get rid of you for good?" Dylan asked, fear shooting through him at the idea of someone harming Allegra.

"Don't worry," Esther said, leveling silent censure at him. "They'd have to find you first. We'll help you come up with a workable plan. I promise. At least there are no headlines about someone kidnapping you."

Dylan frowned, not as convinced as Esther about Allegra's safety, and poured himself a cup of tea. There was something about Allegra that made him want to protect her, to touch, to nip and bite, and her spicy floral scent was driving him crazy.

He couldn't help but acknowledge a fascination with the princess, and if she were any other woman, he'd ask her out. He admired her mental strength. Dylan glanced at her, and a thought occurred. Would she be amiable to a short-term relationship? At the least, it might ease the sexual tension that had sparked from the first moment he saw her. But it wasn't the time to act on those feelings. Allegra had more significant problems, and he didn't want to complicate things. He vowed to be her friend, offering understanding and an open ear.

3

ALLEGRA WOKE TO A sharp knock. She groggily slid from the bed and stumbled over to open the door. Dylan stood there, handsome and sexy, in a forest-green T-shirt and faded jeans.

"Good morning." His grin was sunshiny bright. "Esther had to go to work, and I promised her I'd give you a town tour."

Allegra fought to keep her emotions in line. Amazement filled her at the powerful pull she felt and the yearning to spend time with him. What was it about this wolf?

"That sounds great," she said, aiming for casual. "I guess I'd better get dressed."

"Are you hungry?"

A loud grumble from her stomach supplied the

answer, and she clapped her hands on her hot cheeks.

His eyes twinkled with amusement. "I'll take that as a yes. We'll have breakfast at the cafe." He checked his watch. "Make that brunch."

"Oh! I'm sorry I slept so long. You should've woken me earlier."

"No problem. I'll be in the kitchen, reading the news headlines when you're ready."

Allegra closed the door, dressed in jeans, a cotton shirt, and sneakers, and brushed her hair. As promised, she found Dylan at the kitchen table.

He eyed her with masculine interest and approval. "That was quick."

"My mother used to despair since I've never enjoyed dressing formally. Esther will tell you. I'm much happier in jeans and a T-shirt."

"That's going to make it tricky in your position," Dylan said, guiding her outside.

Allegra laughed, picturing the consternation on the council members' faces. "I figured I'd leave my crown at home today."

Dylan's grin was a thing of beauty, and it took him from handsome to stunning.

"Are you married?" she blurted.

His brow crinkled. "No."

"Why not?" She waved with her right hand, indicating his tall, powerful body. "I mean, I can't see anything wrong with you unless you're hiding extra toes inside those boots of yours." Her gaze drifted up his jeans-clad legs to skim his... Oh, no! She was so not going there.

A delighted expression crossed his face when he opened the door of a black SUV for her. "Were you intimating I might have extra appendages, princess?"

She hurriedly climbed inside and busied herself with the seat belt. Luckily, he didn't expect an answer and closed the door, trotting around the hood to get to the driver's side. Allegra's muscles had almost relaxed when Dylan turned to her with smiling hazel eyes.

"Are you intending to answer? I mean, it's only polite since you started the conversation."

"Something happened to me when I crossed the International Dateline. The traversal broke my verbal filter. That's the only explanation," Allegra said, striving for an earnest tone.

"Is that right?"

"Are you flirting with me?" Allegra's breath caught.

Was that interest in his bright gaze?

"If you need to ask, I must not be doing it right. How about I make the situation clearer for both of us?" Dylan's warm breath sent shivers down Allegra's spine.

He leaned closer, his big hands cupping her face. Allegra's heart pounded so hard she could feel it in her throat. She looked into Dylan's eyes, losing herself in their deep hazel. He was so close now, his lips almost brushing hers.

Without a word, Dylan closed the minuscule gap, capturing her lips in a sensual kiss. Allegra responded eagerly, running her hands through his hair as he deepened the contact, his tongue exploring her mouth.

Lost in their passionate embrace, their bodies melded together, and their lips moved in perfect harmony. Allegra's head spun, responding to Dylan in a way she hadn't for another man. When they eventually separated, the warmth of his lips lingered, and her pulse raced like a wolf running at top speed.

Dylan pressed his forehead against hers, his inhalations heavy and labored. His warm breath tickled her cheek. "Wow," he murmured, his voice husky. "I've wanted to do that since I first saw you."

The kiss left Allegra speechless, her mind spinning. She wanted more, but reality intruded. With a sigh, she pulled away from Dylan and tried to compose herself.

"Let's get going," she murmured, her voice barely above a whisper. "I can't wait to see what this town offers."

Dylan made a grumbly sound. "I'd rather kiss you again, but I did promise to give you a tour."

"You did, and your sister has a formidable temper. You know not to cross her."

Dylan pulled a face. "Is that a threat?"

Allegra pressed her lips together, that cursed heat in her cheeks again. She'd blushed more in front of him than in the entire previous year. But Dylan's presence also gave her a sense of security, liberating her to feel at ease. Bolstered further by this thought, she reached out and touched his knee. His rich forest scent filled her lungs, adding to the attraction simmering through her. He smelled amazing. She wouldn't be averse to rubbing against him and taking on the same scent.

Dylan turned onto the gravel road, and Allegra surveyed the scenery with more interest.

Chestnut-colored cattle grazed in several of the paddocks they passed before reaching the tarmac. She spied two single-level houses, one with two horses lazing in front. Ahead, a bright blue vehicle chugged along the road, and they joined the line of cars behind it.

"Is that a tractor?" Allegra asked in surprise.

"Yes, you get used to meeting farm vehicles since this area is rural. You'll see stock trucks, too."

The town proper was smaller than anything Allegra had conjured in her mind. There was a single main street that they drove along at a snail's pace because it appeared the tractor was traveling in the same direction. Dylan pointed out the school and the community hall. The female-run motor vehicle garage and a dress shop, a superette, the newly opened town bank, and the offices of the vet/shifter doctor.

"You and Esther haven't lived here long. I thought you loved Scotland."

"We did, but we had pack problems. Our alpha fell in love with a feline shifter who lived in Middlemarch. Rory gave us the option of staying on the clan lands in Scotland or following him to Middlemarch. Esther and I gambled on a complete change. We haven't regretted our decision for a moment."

"I wish I could move here, too. It seems peaceful. Instead, I'll need to return to Val-de-Loups and sort out my problems." She heaved out a dispirited sigh.

"Do you have a strategy in mind?"

Allegra pulled a face. "I thought I'd start at the beginning and write a list of what I know, what I suspect, and plausible scenarios to right the wrongs. Who knows? Writing stuff down might jog a brainwave free."

"Your parents and brother didn't die that long ago. Sorry," he added when she winced. He clasped her hand in a brief squeeze of sympathy before withdrawing. "What I was trying to ask in my bumbling, tactless way—was there anything suspicious about their deaths?"

"The police never apprehended their killer. There were no witnesses—at least not credible ones. My parents and Pierre rarely attended the same functions because they liked to visit and discuss matters with a wide range of residents. When they split their duties, they covered more ground."

Dylan parked behind a muddy farm truck and switched off the ignition. "This is the cafe."

Someone had transformed an old house, and its quaint charm was undeniable. Allegra noticed the bike rack outside, filled with several bicycles, and the beautiful rose bushes bearing pink and white blooms edged the path leading to a verandah. Four hanging baskets, full of vibrant purple petunias, swayed in the gentle breeze.

Dylan opened the door and ushered her inside. The scent of coffee and cinnamon floated in the air, the enticing aroma reminding her she hadn't eaten for hours. A blast of conversation battered her sensitive ears, and she couldn't see a single empty table.

Dylan urged her to a counter where a woman with brown hair and a bright, welcoming smile stood, tending to customers. She and Dylan joined the end of the line to wait for their turn.

"I didn't expect it to be so busy." Along with the coffee and cinnamon scents came the musky scent of wolves and, if she wasn't mistaken, feline.

"Dylan," the woman said.

"Hi, Emily, this is Allegra Wolfehart. She went to school with Esther, and she's staying with us for a brief holiday."

"Welcome to Middlemarch and the bedlam that is

my café." Emily's welcoming smile echoed her words. "It's lovely to meet you."

"Emily, any free tables? Allegra and I came for breakfast."

A dark-haired woman spoke from behind them. "Yes, in the garden, if you don't mind playing kids."

"Allegra, this is Tomasine. Allegra is staying with Esther and me," Dylan said to the new arrival.

The doorbell tinkled, and three men stepped inside the cafe.

"You'd better hustle if you want that table," Tomasine said.

"What would you like for breakfast?" Emily asked.

"Two full English breakfasts," Dylan said, checking her reaction for agreement.

"And coffee," Allegra said. "Black for me."

"I'll take a latte, please," Dylan said.

"Go grab the table." Emily noted their requirements on an order pad. "There might be a wait because we're busy with the tour bus passengers."

"No problem, we're not in a hurry," Dylan winked at Allegra.

"Great, we'll bring your meals as soon as they're ready." Emily waved them away and smiled at the men behind them.

Dylan and Allegra headed outside to the garden. It was a grassy patch with several tables and a play area for children. A tall green hedge enclosed the space, and soft music played in the background. Three children were playing with toys while their mothers sat at a nearby table, watching their children and enjoying their coffee.

Dylan and Allegra found a table in a quiet corner and sat. Allegra took a notebook and pen from her bag, intending to start her list. She nibbled on a fingernail, unsure of where to begin.

"You were telling me about your parents," Dylan said.

"Yes." She collected her thoughts. "The police ascertained the shooter's position, but there was precious little other information. Somehow, the shooter vanished. No one saw them, and there was no hard evidence at the site."

"And your brother?"

Allegra drew in a sharp breath. "He took the last shot and lived the longest. I received a phone call but didn't reach the hospital in time."

"Allegra, I'm sorry."

She shrugged because the tightness of her throat prevented her from speaking.

"What made you suspicious about your council?"

"I made decisions at meetings, sometimes overruling the council because I have that power as the princess. The balance in the royal bank account was lower than the books that Pierre kept showed it should be, and lately, we've had a series of mishaps around the chateau. We have inexplicable staff shortages, and minor items have gone missing from rooms. Maybe I'm overreacting."

"But someone shot at you."

"Yes, while I was in the wilderness."

"Someone could've followed you."

"Possibly. I was angry and wasn't paying attention to my surroundings."

Their gazes locked, and Dylan leaned in, his hand resting on her thigh. "You know, Allegra, I'm here for whatever you need."

"Are you trying to make a move on me?" A happy shiver tiptoed down her spine.

He smiled. "Maybe, but I truly want to help."

"I know." She changed the direction of the conversation. "The hardest thing is that I don't know what I'm doing. I've had to learn on the job and go with my gut because tradition means only the heir receives training." And that was one thing she intended to change. The fate of the country shouldn't rest on one person's shoulders. Yes, the council had power, but if her husband or consort stood at her side, they could share the burden.

Until now, there had been an imbalance between the council and Allegra, as they stood on opposite sides of a line. She believed that power needed to be more equitable.

"Perhaps I should stand down and allow the council to rule," she said.

"But if they're up to mischief, that wouldn't change. Your people would still end up royally screwed."

"What alternatives do I have?" She was feeling sorry for herself. This so-called plan of hers was a myth. So far, at least.

"Do you have notes or minutes from the council meetings to help you understand what has happened in the past? Maybe your country's history would provide insight?"

"I've considered that, but the council has the

minutes. When I asked to see them, they told me not to bother my pretty little head. They enjoyed putting me in my place."

Tomasine arrived with their breakfasts, and the conversation turned to more general things while they ate. Dylan glanced over his shoulder and studied the table of two human women and their young children. He turned back to her.

"The shifters in Middlemarch are organizing a run tonight. Want to come with Esther and me? It could be good for you, and I can introduce you to Saber Mitchell."

"That sounds like fun," Allegra said, and it didn't hurt that she'd manage a few quick peeks at Dylan before he shifted.

4

ALLEGRA PULSED WITH EXCITEMENT as she approached the clusters of shifters waiting for the start of the evening run. She walked beside Esther and sensed Dylan following closely behind them while she marveled that leopards, tigers, lions, and wolves lived in harmony in the same community.

The moon hung high in the sky, casting a pale glow on the rugged terrain and the makeshift car park at the rear of an old hay shed. It wasn't quite full yet, but the sight tugged at her and increased her awareness. Luckily, her people shifted at will, and moonlust never affected them, but the full moon always brought a sense of wonder, and she wanted to howl in celebration.

Allegra held back her urge to vocalize, not wanting

to attract attention. This gathering was inspiring with the sense of normalcy she craved for her people. The ability to work together for a better life, improved health, and prosperity. Community was what was missing in Val-des-Loups, and she knew it.

Her parents had ruled well, but the council held too much power. They required fresh blood and new ideas instead of automatically keeping council positions to the same families. Change would be difficult but not impossible. Somehow she needed to confront the enormous challenge ahead.

Dylan nudged her shoulder, his eyes glinting with anticipation. "Ready for this?"

"I'll admit I'm excited. We have nothing like this at home." Allegra grinned at him. She'd stow her epiphany but would drag it out for reexamination later.

"Our lives have become more social here, although felines outnumber the wolves. Mainly black leopards," Esther said and offered a wave and a cheerful greeting to someone in the distance.

A signal sounded, and everyone stopped chatting and turned toward a makeshift platform. A tall man with black hair jumped up and faced the crowd.

"Everyone knows the rules. We leave in smaller groups and monitor your surroundings. It's private land, but unexpected things can happen."

"Let's shift," Esther said, disrobing. Allegra hesitated, aware of Dylan's presence. But that was silly. She had shifted in front of other wolves in the past. Shrugging aside her awareness, she followed Esther's example, rapidly shucking her clothes and setting them aside. She snuck a glance in Dylan's direction. He wasn't staring at her, but wow! She was undoubtedly staring at him. The man had muscles beneath his T-shirt, and she had the crazy urge to close the distance between them and caress every dip and curve.

A muffled snort and a sharp jab in her ribs startled her from her gaping.

"You like my brother," Esther sing-songed.

"Shush." Allegra hurriedly shifted so she didn't have to talk. Her friend would tease her mercilessly now, and it was her fault. She sidled away from Esther as the other wolf nudged her nose, making a sound that communicated a lot. At least this had taken her mind off her problems.

A large black wolf appeared on Allegra's other side

and rubbed against her. Dylan. He was even more gorgeous in his wolf form, and she loved his rich amber scent.

The shifters took off in what looked like family groups, and Allegra paced impatiently, waiting for their turn to leave the meeting point. Adrenaline rushed through her as she finally sprang into motion, the wind whipping through her fur. She could hear the other shifters' yips and muted howls, the felines' grunts, their joy and freedom infectious.

Esther and Dylan ran at her sides up the muddy farm track and into the tree-covered hills. Allegra couldn't help but steal glances at Dylan. His sleek black fur shimmered in the moonlight, and she admired his power and grace. She noticed him eyeing her too, causing anticipation to ripple through her.

They ran for what felt like hours, weaving in and out of trees and leaping over streams. Exhilaration filled Allegra. It was fantastic to be in the present for a change instead of stressing about the future.

Finally, they completed the circuit and arrived back at the old hay shed. Allegra's sides rose and fell rapidly, her breaths coming in pants when she stood back and shifted to her human form.

She claimed her clothes and hurriedly dressed before turning to Esther and Dylan. "Thanks so much for including me. I run as often as possible at home but usually on my own. This run was fun, and it's so nice seeing entire families—even children—joining with the rest of the adults."

Dylan winked at Allegra, admiration in his hazel gaze. "You were amazing out there," he said, his voice filled with genuine respect.

Allegra felt a warm glow of pride at his words. "You weren't too bad yourself."

"Stop flirting in front of me," Esther said, and Allegra thought she was holding back a smile while trying to sound grumpy and disapproving. "I'm starving. Let's get something to eat. At least that might distract me from all your come-hither looks."

They wandered to the back of the shed, where a bulky man and his two teenage assistants were grilling outside.

"Allegra, this is Saber Mitchell, the leader of the Feline Council," Dylan said.

Dylan's hand on the small of her back left Allegra breathless, yet this was the worst time for romance. Her heart gave a physical wrench as her mind forced her to make the only decision possible. Whatever relationship she found with Dylan would end when she left Middlemarch.

"Saber, I'd like to introduce you to Princess Allegra Wolfehart," he said, his tone low and pitched to reach only Saber.

Saber's green eyes widened, but he waited for Dylan to add more.

"Allegra rules a kingdom in Europe. She has had problems and wondered if she could pick your brain. I told her you might offer advice or know someone she could turn to for help."

Saber offered his hand for her to shake. "Come and eat with my family. This isn't the best place for a discussion, but we might manage some privacy. I presume you want to keep the conversation between us?"

Allegra clasped his fingers, impressed by his friendly smile and the subtle power and confidence that emanated from the leopard shifter. The wolves on the council gave her verbal pats on the head and shoved aside her objections or opinions about their decisions. This man held her gaze and treated her as an equal—heady stuff, given her treatment by her fellow wolves at home.

"Thank you. I'd enjoy that very much. I'm here with Esther. We attended boarding school together in Europe and haven't seen each other for almost a year."

"Dylan and Esther are welcome to sit with us. I give you fair warning. Our table will be noisy since my mate Emily is bringing our twin daughters." He gazed upward as if seeking help from the heavens. "My daughters make enough noise for everyone to presume Emily and I have six children."

"I'm sure I'll survive, although I have little experience with children," she said.

"Sometimes I wonder what Emily and I were thinking when we had children," Saber muttered.

Dylan laughed. "I'll tell Emily."

"I'll deny everything." Saber's expression morphed to severe. "My kids are still loveable hellions."

Allegra was about to apologize for Dylan when she spotted the flash of humor in Saber. She barked out a laugh and slapped her hand over her mouth. "Sorry."

Saber chuckled. "That's Emily over there. I'll help her unload the supplies if you grab a table and some meat."

As the night progressed, Allegra mulled over her

conversation with Saber. She absentmindedly twirled a piece of hair around her finger as she pondered her next move.

Dylan had gone to grab more food, leaving her alone at the picnic table. She attempted to soothe her agitated thoughts. She couldn't shake the sense there was more to her family's assassination than what met the eye. Her mind drifted over the last month and her actions, then came to an abrupt full stop.

Wow! *The runes.* Her brother had ordered her to hide them, but why had he been so insistent? She pictured the flat box he'd given her in her mind's eye. Papers. There had *been* papers at the bottom beneath the runes. Pierre had been vehement that she kept the box safe and didn't discuss it with anyone. Yeah, she'd check out the runes as soon as she returned home.

Allegra experienced a pang of regret. She should've asked more, but history and things concerning Val-des-Loups hadn't stirred her interest then. Now, she had questions and no one to ask them of—at least, no one she could trust. The council likely hid away anything of importance in the chateau, but perhaps they'd missed something. She made a mental note to search through her belongings the next chance she got.

After they finished eating, Dylan suggested they head home. Allegra couldn't help but experience a newfound determination as they walked back to their vehicle. She intended to investigate her family's assassination, no matter what it took, and most of all, she wanted to effect change to improve the lives of Val-des-Loups' citizens.

Esther had disappeared to spend time with another group, and Allegra and Dylan stopped to speak with her.

"Go home without me," she said.

Brother and sister exchanged a look, and Allegra intercepted Dylan's faint incline of the head. Allegra would've said more, but Dylan took her arm and propelled her away.

"What? I'm not allowed to tease Esther. She's quite happy to give me a hard time."

"Has it crossed your mind that Esther might have intentionally left us alone?"

"You want privacy with me?" Allegra stopped walking, jerking to him in surprise. What she saw in his face made her burn—in a good way.

She hadn't had a date for... Wow, three years. Life at

the chateau was like living inside a fishbowl, and she refused the gossip for herself or any man she liked, so she'd abstained.

Now... Dylan tempted her.

"Nothing to say about that?"

"I must return to Val-des-Loups. This is a break to get my head together, devise a plan to survive, and help my people," she stated, sticking to the facts despite her inner struggle. They had no future when they lived on different sides of the world.

His expression went hard and reading it—impossible. She blinked, but that implacable visage remained.

"Let's go," he said.

It was a short drive to Esther and Dylan's home, and they accomplished the journey without a single word spoken. The silence zinged with tension rather than their outward trip's ease and laughter.

Dylan pulled up outside his home and slid her a sideways glance. "Suppose I said I didn't care about the future? What if I told you I only want now?"

"A concise explanation, please, so I understand your meaning."

"I want you," he said, and his words were stark and

unhappy.

"You don't seem pleased about that."

"Because I'm cursing at the fuckin' timing. My life is here in Middlemarch. I've made a commitment to the town and our pack. Your life is in Val-des-Loups. You have your own set of obligations. But that doesn't stop my wolf from craving you. I want to strip off every item of clothing and mold your shape with my hands. I'll lick and kiss you. Slide my cock into your receptive and sexy body. Tell me you don't want that either."

Allegra closed her eyes, every inhalation full of his amber, musky scent. The fragrance of the outdoors clung to his skin, too, and it was so enticing.

"Allegra?"

Her breath whooshed out. "Yes."

5

DYLAN BREATHED OUT A sigh of relief. He hadn't been able to stop thinking about Allegra all night, and he'd subtly laid claims of ownership with the other Middlemarch males. No doubt he'd score a heap of teasing from his friends, but in this instant, he didn't give a fuck. When Allegra had shifted, he'd stared, and now he'd imprinted every inch of her beautiful body on his mind.

God, he desired her so much that his hands trembled. If he wasn't holding onto the steering wheel, this would be apparent. Dylan schooled his body to obedience and climbed from the vehicle. By the time he rounded the hood, Allegra had exited the SUV and stood waiting for him.

He extended his hand, and she gripped it without

hesitation. Though her hand was small, he knew not to underestimate her strength. Allegra possessed a steel backbone and would undoubtedly become an influential leader once she resolved the issues in her kingdom. However, he pushed these thoughts to the recesses of his mind.

Take what you can get. Use this valuable time with Allegra—the privacy that Esther has given you.

He tugged Allegra toward the rear door and unlocked it, standing aside to usher her indoors. "Would you like a drink?"

"No thanks. I need a shower."

Disappointment seared him. Had he misunderstood?

Allegra glanced over her shoulder. "I'll need someone to scrub my back. Your shower is roomy enough for two."

Relief almost took him out at the knees. "You start. I'll be there shortly." He needed to give himself a talking to and tell his wolf to calm the hell down. *There would be no biting or marking.* "Ground rules," he murmured and relocked the door. Although this was a safe community, he wanted to protect Allegra. A mystery gunman had shot at her, and who knew if they'd followed her to Middlemarch.

The shower was running when he entered the bathroom, orange-scented steam billowing out to greet him. He'd already removed his boots, and now, he shucked his socks, T-shirt, jeans, and underwear. He crossed the tiled floor and stared at her, all pink skin and gorgeous curves.

Dylan stepped into the stall, and she turned to him, her brows rising.

"You took so long I thought you'd changed your mind," she said with a genuine smile that reeled him in.

He liked that she didn't try to hide any part of her body, and that teasing smile did things to his insides, making his stomach swoop and swirl. She was such an odd mixture of siren and innocent, and he found her beguiling.

The steam was thick and enveloped them in a cocoon of warmth and privacy. He stood just a few feet away from her, his heart racing. Her stunning lake-blue eyes devoured him with an intensity that left him weirdly vulnerable and exposed. She studied him with a hunger, her gaze scouring his body as if she wanted to commit every contour to memory. His palms turned sweaty as he watched her intently, barely able to contain his excitement.

This woman.

It was difficult to believe they'd first met the previous day. Every part of him, human and wolf, begged him, ordered him to take her. "You are so beautiful. I thought so when I met you at the airport, but now—you're simply stunning."

Her hair cascaded down her back like a curtain of black silk, glistening with water droplets from the showerhead above them. His gaze followed her curves as she moved closer until only inches separated them.

Dylan swallowed, the heat radiating off her skin and her saucy smile communicating the same hunger that pulsed through him. Her captivating scent drew him. He looked into those bright blue eyes that held an unspoken desire, a passion that threatened to consume them both. Allegra closed the scant distance between them, and their bodies brushed, sending shivers down his spine.

"Kiss me."

He had no problem with her suggestion. Dylan leaned in and captured Allegra's lips with his, tasting the warmth of her mouth and exploring her with a fervor that left them breathless. His hands roamed her curves, tracing the softness of her skin, and he reveled in her moan of pleasure.

The water washed over them, creating a sensual rhythm that matched the movements of their bodies. Consumed by their common desire, they were lost in the moment.

"This isn't getting us clean," he murmured finally.

"I borrowed Esther's shower gel and washed away the mud from our run before you arrived."

"Look at you, Miss Efficient."

She pressed a quick kiss to his mouth and pulled away to grab the shower loofah. After squirting a dollop of orange-scented shower gel on it, she said, "Turn around, and I'll do your back."

Like a robot, he turned and placed his palms against the tiled wall, his eyes closing at the hard pressure of her touch. She used a steady force, swirling the loofah across his back and lower over his butt. Predictably, his cock took notice, and Dylan barely held back his groan of pleasure. Allegra taking care of him was tenfold better than his brisk cleaning sessions.

"Done," she said after washing the back of each thigh and calf. "I'll let you do the front."

He turned and stole a kiss before accepting the loofah from her. He made quick work of the job, his gaze catching hers as he rinsed the scrubber and hung it on a hook to dry.

Then he kissed her, tracing her mouth with the tip of his tongue. The kiss was electric and powerful, sending shockwaves through him as Allegra melted into his embrace. Right now, he felt alive, part of something bigger than himself. Dylan lost himself in her clinch and a thrill electrified every part of him. Allegra's lips moved against his hungrily, heightening Dylan's wolf senses. Scent. Touch. Hearing.

They pulled apart and stared at each other in wonder.

"The water is getting cold," he said.

"Mr. Obvious," she teased, then grew serious. "Are we sharing a bedroom tonight?"

"If that's what you want."

"Yes."

Dylan turned off the water and opened the door. He reached for a towel and handed it to her before grabbing one for himself. He rapidly dried off before hanging up the bath linen. Dylan checked Allegra's expression, relaxing on seeing the same desire that burned within him.

Without a word, they left the bathroom and headed to the bedroom. Dylan took charge, guiding Allegra to the bed and laying her down gently.

Electricity charged the air and made his skin tingle. His wolfish senses caught the *boom-boom-boom* of her wildly beating heart and her quickened breathing. The overpowering urge to kiss her again was impossible to resist.

"You have me twisted up like a pretzel." He leaned in to nuzzle her neck, then nibbled on her earlobe, thrilled at her soft moan. He brushed the tips of his fingers along her collarbone, taking his sweet time and hopefully building the anticipation.

"Your skin is soft." He skated his thumb against the side of one breast.

"I love the drag of your fingers," she whispered, her eyes, darker in hue now, on him.

"Working with wood is hard on the hands," he said, watching her nipple pull to a hard nub. "So pretty."

He leaned over and sucked her nipple into his mouth. He drew hard and savored her loud moan.

"Like that, do you?"

"I enjoy everything you do. Again." She clasped his

head and forced it back down.

Her fingers laced in his hair, and a rough growl vibrated in his chest. He wanted everything with her.

"I wanted to go slow and explore every part of you. You're not making this easy."

Allegra nodded, her kiss-swollen lips twitching. "Who said I wanted easy or slow? You should never assume."

"What do you want then?"

"I want you to fuck me. Help me drown in pleasure, so I forget my troubles."

Her bluntness took him aback, even though he'd asked her what she wanted. The thing was, whatever was up with his wolf was more than he'd ever imagined. He didn't want to hurry or take her just for pleasure, for the pure fun of sexual release. He wanted more.

His problem.

He knew that, but the knowledge didn't help him now.

Resolved, he lowered his head to take her mouth, his hand cupping her breast. He tweaked the nipple, giving her a hint of pain. When he glanced up to check her reaction, her eyes filled with a hunger that matched his own. He parted her legs with his thigh, going faster than he wanted. Damn, if he had limited time with her, he wanted memories to keep him warm when he was alone again.

A visual.

Without thinking twice, he turned onto his back so he lay flat. He lifted Allegra over him and smiled at her shocked visage.

"Take what you want. Show me what you like."

Sudden enthusiasm glowed in her. "I can do that."

She arranged herself, her hand curling around his aching erection. Allegra lifted and guided his cock to her, sinking down. His heart beat faster, harder, and he watched her expression as her flesh parted to let him slide deeper. She stilled, her sheath tightening and squeezing him.

"I thought you wanted to hurry."

"I'm getting there." Her smile slid into a teasing category.

But to his relief, she rose again, dragging his shaft against her center in a sinful massage. His gaze locked with hers, pleasure frisking every nerve ending. She rode him slowly, teasing before escalating her speed.

Allegra threw her head back, mesmerizing him with

her innate sensuality. She bounced on him, her tight sheath caressing his shaft and leaving him shaking. Her thighs tensed, her grip on his cock tightened, and Allegra screamed his name. Her pussy clenched around him, and he groaned as he surged into her, caught in the rhythm of her body, the pleasure building in him. Then her orgasm triggered his, and he shot his seed, his heart racing impossibly fast.

Dylan held her close, and he listened to her erratic breathing. He raised a hand and tilted her head to meet his gaze. "I'm not done with you. Relax, we're just beginning."

"I'll hold you to it," she said, her voice breathless.

"I can't wait." Dylan shifted his weight to his side and claimed her mouth, his desire still not sated. He wanted more and took her in a torrid kiss. Her lips were wet and luscious and so, so soft. He kissed her deeply, using his tongue to taste her fully. Her fingers slid between their bodies and lightly cupped his balls, teasing him.

"Again?" he asked.

"Again," she agreed.

"You're temptation on two legs," he declared, already rising. He claimed her mouth again, not giving her time to think.

Dylan lifted her and placed her on the pillows. He settled between her parted thighs and pushed into her again, loving her wet, slick entrance.

Allegra arched up to meet him, and he sank deeper.

"We haven't used condoms," he said.

"I'm on birth control. Sometimes, it's handy being a werewolf because we don't have the same sexual worries as humans." She wrinkled her nose at him. "And at other times, it's a pain in the butt."

His gaze narrowed. "Esther and I have a good life in Middlemarch. Our life in the Highlands wasn't peaceful, and I'm glad Rory settled here."

"Esther has mentioned little about living in Scotland."

"She didn't know the worst of it because she was away at boarding school. I thought it was silly of my parents to send her, but ultimately, I was grateful because it kept her away from the drama. This discussion is a mood killer. I'd rather make love to you."

"I'm not stopping you."

"Excellent." He halted further conversation by kissing her. He thrust, his hands skimming her breasts and hips. She writhed beneath his weight, silently enticing him to increase his pace. Sensual energy coursed between them, and he pushed deeper. A quick punch of heat grasped him, and he shuddered, his balls tingling in a precursor of climax. He pistoned his hips, and Allegra groaned.

"Yes!" She lifted into his next stroke. Her sex spasmed around his girth, and he growled his pleasure. The familiar and welcome low pressure gathered. He nipped her earlobe, and she came.

Heat swirled through him, driving up his cock as he climaxed. They were both breathing hard and held each other as they returned to Earth.

"Thank you. That was amazing."

Dylan bit back his instinctive words. He didn't want her to thank him. He wanted her to stay in Middlemarch. His wolf half certainly approved of the idea, and he was beginning to think she might be his mate. He'd heard finding a mate was sudden, the wolf sensing the rightness of being with their other half. It had been an instant interest with him. He thought she returned the sentiment, but she had to go home.

He held back his frustration, his sigh of unhappiness. They had a few more days before she flew home. He could spend time with Allegra and help her as much as possible. If he was lucky, she might start seeing him in a different light.

"Let's get under the covers before we get cold," he said.

"I'm too lazy to move."

"No problem." He clambered off the bed and dragged back the quilt, then lifted and laid her down again. Moments later, he joined her. "Sleep," he whispered, snuggling her close. As her breathing gradually became slow and steady, he smiled and shut his eyes, feeling happier than he had in a long time.

6

ALLEGRA STIRRED AND SLOWLY came awake. She spent a panicked moment trying to remember what had happened the previous night and where she was until she sensed a weight in the bed beside her. Dylan lay on his side, his face relaxed in slumber, his warm amber scent filling her every breath.

Relaxing, she swallowed to moisten her mouth and decided she needed water. Allegra inched out of bed, her gaze glued to Dylan's sleeping form as she tiptoed across the room. A blush heated her cheeks because she was skulking around as if she'd done something wrong. Stupid, really. The night chill amplified each creak from the floorboards, but Dylan didn't stir. In the kitchen, she opened a cupboard, grabbed a glass, and stretched to reach the tap. After filling it with cold water, she took a sip and relished its refreshing taste.

As she drank, she gazed out the window, taking in the wild and untamed gardens surrounding the house. The thick trees and undergrowth obscured her view beyond the garden's edge, even in the moonlight. A chill ran down her spine without warning, and she had the distinct sensation of being watched.

She turned around, her heart racing, gaze searching the darkness through another window. But no one was there. She shook her head, chalking her nervousness up to fatigue and stress from the last week.

It was her imagination.

She sipped water and turned to the first window. She could still see nothing except the overgrown plants, but the feeling of an observer persisted, and she couldn't shake it. Allegra set her glass on the counter and walked to a different window, peering into the darkness. This kitchen felt like a goldfish bowl with its myriad windows. She hadn't switched on lights because, with her wolfish senses, she didn't need the extra illumination. She strained her eyes to spot anything moving in the shadows that might account for her weird intuition of a Peeping Tom.

A branch snapped in the distance, and she jumped, a tiny squeak escaping her. She stepped back, her heart pounding, her hand pressed to her chest.

Allegra's mind raced. Had someone followed her from Val-des-Loups? Or was an animal roaming outside?

Her gaze darted around the kitchen, searching for a weapon, and she reached for a knife from the counter. She told herself it was her imagination, but her jittery nerves and unease lingered.

She remained by the window, keeping a watchful eye on the garden. Eventually, the prickling sensation subsided, and Allegra returned to bed. Even as she lay next to Dylan, she couldn't shake the notion that someone or something had been watching her.

Her mind jumped from one problem to another, refusing to settle, refusing to allow her to sink back into sleep. She'd intended to check on the runes and see if the papers inside the box were lining or if her memory was correct and the pages held valuable information. No time like the present, especially since she couldn't sleep.

Allegra slid out of bed again, and thankfully, Dylan didn't stir. She must've tired him out and looked forward to teasing him tomorrow. She hurried to the bedroom she shared with Esther, drew the curtains, turned on the light, and closed the door to avoid disturbing Dylan with the brightness.

Her pulse raced as she plonked on the bed in Esther's bedroom and drew up her feet to sit cross-legged. A chill ran through her, and she thanked the instinct that had suggested she screen the windows. Still, she glanced around before retrieving the flat box, which held the runes, from under a stack of books.

Once again, she couldn't shake the edginess that assailed her—the prickling sensation on her skin, like tiny needles jabbing her from the inside out. If she had been in her wolf form, the fur along her spine would stand to attention. But despite the primitive warning signs, the bedroom was marginally safer than the kitchen with fewer windows.

Allegra stared at the pale blue box, grubby from years of handling. It was the size of a small hardback book. Unaccountably, her hand trembled, and a wash of stark fear gripped her. What if this box meant nothing, and her memory of the conversation with Pierre resulted from teenage exaggeration? It was possible. She bit her lip, trying to remember the exact words her brother had used. He'd come to her room early one morning on the day she'd been leaving to head back to boarding school in France.

What had he told her?

Her brow knit as she concentrated. He'd said their father had given the runes to him, and he was passing them on to her. They were old but not toys, and he'd opened the lid to show her the contents. She remembered disappointment because boys, music, and makeup had held more interest. A rueful smile curved her lips. She'd been a typical teen. Pierre had instructed her to keep them secure, and when she turned twenty-five, he'd explain their history.

And this wasn't progressing with her investigation. It was full-out procrastination.

Allegra gulped and unfastened the rusty clasp on the side that kept the box closed. She lifted the lid and scrutinized the black runes.

The eight runes were finely crafted and carved from black onyx. Each bore a unique symbol etched into its surface. She picked up each one, scrutinizing them. The heavy stones felt cool in Allegra's hand and possessed a strange energy that coiled through her body and settled deep in her bones. The sensation was dizzying and off-putting at first, but she soon became accustomed to the pulse and zing, finding it strangely welcoming. She ran her finger along each edge, testing the intricate pattern around the borders and the tiny divots in the glassy surface of the stone.

Allegra felt a connection she couldn't explain, as though they were calling her, deepening the mystery because she'd recalled touching them when Pierre gave them to her. She'd have remembered if she'd experienced this familiarity. She gnawed her bottom lip and peered at the runes in her palm. The symbols meant nothing, but she could research the meanings online or at a library.

She set the arcane glyphs aside and paid closer attention to the box's lining. Beneath the top layer of tissue paper, she glimpsed pages bearing words written in ink. Ah! Her memories hadn't played her false.

With trembling fingers, she carefully unfolded the pages from the box. A white envelope fell out, but she set it aside to read the first page.

The Val-des-Loups Prophecy

Huh? What prophecy? She'd never heard of

anything like this concerning the kingdom. Shaking her head, she read further.

In a kingdom long forgotten,
Where the bloodline was begotten,
Runes were cast, ancient and old,
To choose a ruler with a heart of gold.

Their power great, their magic strong,
Each one waiting to belong,
To the one with royal blood,
The heir of Val-des-Loups destined and good.

But the runes will not bind,
Unless the true heir they find,
Their bond will bring prosperity,
To a kingdom once lost in obscurity.

So heed this warning, all who dare,
Only the rightful ruler shall bear,
The magic of the ancient runes,
And reign over the kingdom until they pass to the next
heir.

For when the prophecy is fulfilled,
And the true leader is skilled,
Val-des-Loups will rise again,
And its people will rejoice and sing.

With the runes at their side,
And the kingdom as their guide,
The true heir will bring forth an age,
Of prosperity, peace, and sage.

So heed the call, oh chosen one,
Your destiny has just begun,
To rule with honor, love, and might,
And guide Val-des-Loups to a future bright.

Her mouth agape, Allegra stared at the words in shock. Her parents had never mentioned a prophecy. She reread the verses, trying to make sense of them.

Allegra reached for the envelope, her heart beating faster when she noticed her brother's handwriting and her name on the outside. She swallowed and used her thumb to open the flap. She extracted the single page, her eyes misting. He was ten years older than her but had always played with her when she was little. She'd loved him and missed him like crazy.

"Okay, Pierre. Why are you writing secret letters to me?"

She started reading.

Dear Allegra,

I hope this letter finds you well. As you know, I gave you the runes to keep safe and promised to tell you their history when you turn twenty-five. I got the sense you weren't interested, and that was fine. At sixteen years of age, you shouldn't need to worry about the affairs of Val-des-Loups. That is our parents' job and now mine.

Lately, something has been bothering me, and I can't shake this gut instinct that I must tell you everything now. This goes against the tradition of our line, but it feels like something is about to happen. I want to make sure you're prepared for whatever comes your way.

The runes are not just ordinary stones with inscriptions on them. Our ancestor received them when he helped an elderly woman rebuild her home after a storm when no one else would aid her, and she imbued them with an ancient power that goes beyond our understanding, or so the oral story goes.

The prophecy speaks of a remarkable ruler who will bring prosperity to our kingdom. Only someone with royal blood can bond with the runes; that person is you, Allegra. I believe our parents undervalue your abilities. They sent you to boarding school because they were busy and couldn't handle your high spirits. That was the line they gave me, but if something has happened to me, you are the rightful heir to the throne of Val-des-Loups.

We must use the runes for the good of our people. They can bring about much-needed prosperity when held in the right royal hands. I don't know what the future holds, but our family and kingdom will face significant challenges. The current council members may not have our best interests at heart, and they may try to undermine our parents' rule. You must be careful, Allegra. Keep the runes hidden until the time comes when you can claim your rightful place as the ruler of Val-des-Loups.

Remember, Allegra, you are not alone. You have the

glyph's strength and our courageous people. Be a great queen and prioritize citizens. Our family has always served the kingdom honorably and with dignity. Do the same.

Take care, Allegra.

Your loving brother,

Pierre

A thick lump formed in Allegra's throat as she reread Pierre's letter twice. It was true her parents had been at a loss with her, and she had acted up, exploring the kingdom, and visiting places she shouldn't. After consulting with the council, her parents had sent her to boarding school for a year, which ended up extending to three years in Europe.

At first, Allegra had hated every moment of her stay. The teachers had acted mean and stern, and their discipline was diabolically clever and tailored to suit the occasion. She'd jumped into scrapes and mostly avoided punishment. Her life had improved once she'd met Esther. With Esther as her companion, she'd grown confident and learned to embrace her adventurous side.

"Thanks to Esther, I grew into my skin," Allegra murmured, the mental trip to the past bringing pain and pleasure.

"What are you doing?"

Allegra jolted, her foot knocking the symbols together with a musical clack. She thumped the middle of her chest and willed her heart to jump back into the correct position.

"Allegra?" Dylan stalked into the bedroom, his chest bare and a pair of track pants covering his lower half.

"Sorry, I couldn't sleep. I'd meant to inspect the runes when we arrived home after the run, but I got sidetracked."

"You should've woken me," he said, his tone softer now that worry had burned away.

"You were tired. I had a drink of water and came here. Nothing dangerous."

"As long as you have no regrets about us." His gaze pierced her, communicating a little of his anxiety in the tenseness of his shoulders.

"Not a single one." Allegra blew him a kiss. "I was

thinking about Esther and how we used to get into trouble at school. Gradually, we learned to be sneakier and stopped getting caught. The humans running the school were no match for us."

Dylan laughed, his features shining with delight. "I heard about your escapades in Esther's letters. I just laughed because I knew she could handle most of the trouble."

"Huh! Your sister was way worse than me."

Dylan's attention went to the runes on the bedcovers. "Are those the glyphs you mentioned?"

"Yeah, according to the papers I found with them, these are part of a prophecy that mentions me indirectly and the kingdom of Val-des-Loups."

"Really? Do you think it's real?"

"I don't know," Allegra said. "Things aren't going well. The council is out of control, and when I think back, affairs went wrong after my parents and Pierre died."

"What's next?" Curiosity blazed in him.

"I might go back to bed for more sleep."

A grin spread over his features. "Would you like company?"

7

THE FOLLOWING DAY WAS a late start, and Esther's noisy arrival woke them shortly before nine. Dylan groaned softly, the sound close to her ear. "Does she need to stomp around like an elephant? She's a wolf shifter. She knows how to sneak," he muttered.

Allegra bit back her grin. Esther understood precisely what she was doing. "She's trying to flush us out to interrogate one or both of us. I've been through this before."

"I do not want to hear about your past boyfriends."

"Fair enough. I know you're not married, but you don't have a girlfriend, do you?"

He bolted upright in the bed and glared at her. "Shouldn't we have had that conversation before getting into bed together?" His hair stood on end.

So cute.

"I don't have a girlfriend or lover, and I resent you for implying I might."

She fought back inappropriate laughter as he poked her in the ribs.

Allegra moved out of reach. "Two men have fooled me before, so I should've asked earlier, but you distracted me."

He stared at her for a beat longer. "Two guys?"

"Yeah."

"Arseholes," he muttered.

In the kitchen, a phone rang. The ringing ceased after four rings, then footsteps approached Dylan's bedroom. A tap sounded.

"It's Saber Mitchell," Esther called. "He wants to speak with you."

Dylan hopped off the bed and swung open the door, grasping for the phone. With it in hand, he shoved his sister back and shut the door in her face.

"Rude. Allegra, do you want coffee?"

"Please. I won't be long."

"I will interrogate you," Esther warned through the door.

"Where were you last night?" Allegra countered.

Silence.

"Maybe I'll hold off on the questions. For now," Esther said.

Dylan gave Allegra a thumbs-up sign and spoke into his phone. "How can I help you, Saber?"

"I'm helping you," Saber said. "I spoke to Leo and Isabella. Isabella has loads of contacts in Europe. She told me to tell you she'll meet you at the café for breakfast. She is helping Emily this morning."

"That's great. What time?"

"ASAP," Saber said.

"Okay. Thanks, Saber. We appreciate it." Dylan turned to Allegra, who was busy searching for something to wear since her clothes were in Esther's room.

"Did you get that?"

"Yes. Is this Isabella trustworthy?"

"She's married to one of Saber's brothers. If Saber recommends we speak with her, I'm inclined to trust her. Saber wouldn't steer you wrong."

"I'll need to do the walk of shame," Allegra announced. "I need clothes."

Dylan huffed out a breath. "Esther spent the night with Alex. At least, that's what I assume. I should play the big brother card and ask her what she is doing hanging around with a leopard and sharing his bed." He spoke loudly, and a wolfish growl resounded from the kitchen.

"I'll wash and get dressed," Allegra said. "Won't be long."

When Allegra entered five minutes later, Dylan and Esther sat at the table, hands cupping mugs of coffee. The radio played a lively song Allegra hadn't heard before.

"Good morning." She poured herself a coffee into the mug sitting ready for her.

"So, you and my brother, huh?" Esther said, waggling her brows.

"He's very sexy. Very handsome and charming. I couldn't help myself."

"Thank you," Dylan said.

"Oh, please." Esther emitted a choking sound.

Allegra laughed and took her first sip of coffee. She lifted her gaze and stared out the window. "Before we leave for the café, I'd like to scout around the house. Last night, I had trouble sleeping and came to the kitchen for water. I didn't turn on any lights, but I had a weird feeling that someone was watching me. It could've been my imagination."

Dylan's eyes narrowed, and he set down his coffee mug. "Let's go check it out." When Esther stood, too, Dylan halted. "Esther, maybe stay here and watch for anything suspicious. Whoever Allegra sensed might still be there. You can call the cops or Saber if we get into trouble."

Esther's expression turned serious, and she nodded. "Got it but be careful. Wait, take your phone with you."

"It might be nothing," Allegra said.

"And it may be something," Esther said. "You and Dylan should investigate."

"You thought someone was in the garden, near the kitchen?" Dylan asked.

"Yes."

"Okay, we'll go through the back and search for footprints or anything else that grabs our attention."

Allegra followed Dylan as he led the way out the house's rear door. The bright sunshine had her blinking rapidly before her eyes adjusted to the light.

They moved silently, each step deliberate and cautious as they walked through the overgrown garden. Allegra had to admit she was glad Dylan was by her side. His presence was calming, giving her confidence that they could handle whatever they might find.

She inhaled, and her senses filled with greenery and fresh air. Nothing out of place. "It was hard to see in the dark. It was more a frisson of awareness that someone or something was out here."

"Can you sense anyone now?"

"No, but I'd like to search by those trees over there."

Dylan nodded, and they made their way toward the trees. Allegra's gaze darted to her left, and a wave of familiarity washed over her. She grabbed Dylan's arm, halting him mid-stride, and pressed her finger to her lips. Inhaling deeply, she tried to identify the scent that had caught her attention while the wind rustled through the leaves.

Allegra stepped forward, following her instincts. As she got closer, she saw something glinting in the sunlight. She crept closer and, to her surprise, spotted a dagger lying on the ground. She bent down to inspect the weapon. Intricate carvings covered the hilt—a silver image of a monster's head and a coiled serpent. The blade was sharp and deadly. It smelled of iron and copper and stagnant water. It reeked of death.

She breathed deeply, trying to locate the scent of the person who'd left or dropped the dagger.

Dylan's eyes widened. "That's no ordinary weapon. It's made of silver. This can only mean one thing."

"The council," Allegra said, her tone ominous. "It's got to be. They're getting bolder and aren't afraid to leave their mark and send a message. They're trying to scare me or at least send a warning that they mean business." She swallowed hard, unable to tear her gaze from the serpent and the dangerously sharp blade. Did they have knowledge of the runes? Were they waiting for the right moment to kill her or toying with her as a cat did its prey? "I don't get a sense of the blade's owner."

Dylan nodded grimly. "No, and that's odd. We need to take care. If they followed you here or arranged someone to trail you, they'll probably use any means necessary to take you down."

Allegra clenched her jaw. "I won't let them. I'll fight with everything I have. This is my birthright we're talking about. Val-des-Loups citizens deserve the best—a ruler who will battle for them. One who doesn't give in to greed."

Dylan put a hand on her shoulder and squeezed in silent comfort. "You're strong and capable. But we can't do this alone. We need allies."

Allegra, seeing the sense of this, nodded in agreement. "We're still going to meet Isabella, right? That might be my best bet. Heck, I don't have many options. If Isabella has connections in Europe, then I say use them." She wondered how much this might cost and cringed inwardly. Somehow, she'd find the money. It was worth it if it meant saving the land and her people. Somehow, she'd make this work.

Dylan gave her a small smile. "Then let's go meet her."

"This is dangerous, Dylan. You don't have to take on my fight."

"I want to. At the very least, we're friends, and that's what friends do."

Allegra experienced a sudden sinking sensation in her stomach. Friends, yes. But she wanted more time with Dylan, since he appealed to her on every level. Why did her life have to be in a process of upheaval when she met someone she liked a lot?

Dylan's phone rang, interrupting her reverie.

"Is everything all right out there? Do I need to call

someone?" Esther asked.

"We're coming inside," Dylan said. "We'll explain everything soon." He hung up and dialed Saber. "Saber, I don't have Isabella's number, but we're running late. We'll leave home in ten minutes. Can you let Isabella know?"

"Anything wrong?" Saber asked, his tone sharp.

"Someone left a message for us overnight. At least, that's what we think."

"Do you need help?" Saber asked.

"They've gone. Tracking will be difficult because their scent is weak," Dylan said.

"I'll contact Isabella." Saber hung up.

"Do you recognize the dagger?" Esther asked once they'd explained what they'd seen and found.

"No, although there's something familiar about it. My father was a collector, and it may be from one of his collections. I donated everything to the local museum. The head housekeeper offered to liaise with the curator for me, and I thought nothing of it."

"Esther, maybe we shouldn't leave you alone in the house. You should come with us," Dylan said.

"I'd feel better if I knew you were safe," Allegra agreed before her friend could argue.

The busy morning rush had passed when they arrived at Storm in a Teacup café.

"Isabella's behind the counter," Dylan whispered. "I'll order breakfast. You sit in the corner to monitor the café and any new arrivals."

Esther and Allegra navigated the tables and remaining customers, finally reaching a vacant one in the far corner.

"I didn't expect a glamorous blonde," Allegra said.

"Isabella is gorgeous, isn't she? She teaches self-defense and fitness classes at the community hall." Esther leaned closer to Allegra. "Rumor says she used to be an assassin, but I don't know if that's true."

"It's true," a feminine voice said from behind them. "Saber thought I might assist you, or at least my contacts. He told me you come from Val-des-Loups. I visited once. Your country is beautiful."

"Thank you," Allegra said, envious of Isabella's beautiful violet eyes.

"All right. I have half an hour. Tell me everything."

After an encouraging nod from Dylan and another from Esther, Allegra told Isabella about the assassination of her parents and her brother, the problems she'd experienced with the council, and someone shooting at her. She finished with a description of the runes, a precis of the letter Pierre had written, plus details of the silver dagger they'd discovered this morning.

"Wow," Isabella said. "You think the council wants to rule the kingdom, and they're willing to dispose of you in any way they can to gain control?"

"Yes, but I'm unsure if they are aware of the runes."

"Do you believe what your brother wrote in his letter?"

"When I picked them up last night, I felt power and magic, so yes, I believe they're an important part of what is happening."

"But I thought your parents were the king and queen, and Pierre, your brother, only helped when necessary?" Esther said.

"No, Pierre worked for the kingdom for years, so if he told me to hide the runes, maybe they needed to be at the chateau. Nothing changed until my brother died. I won't know for sure unless I learn anything from my research today."

Isabella listened intently, nodding as Allegra spoke. When she finished, Isabella leaned back in her chair and thoughtfully tapped her fingers on the table.

"Something smells fishy," she said. "And you're in danger if someone is loitering around your house. I might have a way to find help."

Allegra felt a spark of hope. "What do you mean?"

"I have a European contact. He's part of an organization that deals with supernatural threats. They're based in France, and they have many resources at their disposal. They might even help you figure out what those runes mean."

"That sounds amazing." Dylan leaned forward. "But how would we even contact them?"

Isabella spoke up. "I'll make a call. I know the guy who runs the organization. He owes me a favor or two. I'll see what I can do."

"And our loiterer?" Esther asked.

"Saber is concerned about that. We thought it best to report this to the local cops," Isabella said.

Allegra gasped. "But I thought they were humans. Esther, no Dylan. Didn't you mention that during the tour of Middlemarch?"

Isabella raised her hand. "They're human but have shifter mates. I suggest that Esther and Allegra have a night in while Dylan meets us and helps with surveillance. Our cops, my husband Leo, Dylan, and

I will stake out your place tonight. If your watcher was there last evening, they might return. We'll also check out any strangers. If our lurker comes from your kingdom, they'll need to stay somewhere local. We'll reconnoiter today and try to find them."

Dylan frowned. "Do you think they'll hang around Middlemarch?"

"Possibly." Isabella's gaze turned thoughtful. "It's worth a shot. We'll keep you safe, Allegra. I promise."

Allegra's heart swelled with gratitude. She'd had no one to help her at home, leaving her vulnerable, but now, with Isabella, Esther, and Dylan by her side, she had a chance of survival.

"Thank you," she whispered.

Isabella squeezed Allegra's hand. "We've got this. Ah, here's your breakfast. I'll leave you to eat in peace and start the process from my side. Dylan, I'll call you about tonight's stakeout." She strode to the counter, spoke briefly with Emily, and disappeared out the back.

The aroma of eggs, bacon, and freshly brewed coffee wafted through the air as she, Esther, and Dylan dug into their meals. Plumes of steam rose from her cheese omelet. As they savored each bite, they discussed the possibilities of what to do next.

One thing suddenly occurred to Allegra, and her blood ran cold. She'd left the runes and papers on the nightstand in Esther's room. What if someone broke into the house before they returned home?

8

ALLEGRA'S HEART KNOCKED SO hard against her ribs that her brain rattled. *Stupid. Stupid. Stupid.* She tore from Dylan's vehicle, scarcely waiting for him to come to a stop.

"Allegra, wait," Esther called.

"You don't have a key." Dylan's words dragged Allegra to an impatient halt.

Allegra fidgeted while Dylan rummaged in his pocket and produced a key. When the door opened, a wave of lemon furniture polish greeted them. Allegra rushed inside, past the living room, dining room, and kitchen, to Esther's bedroom. She burst through the doorway, fear a beast writhing in her gut. The box holding the runes and letters remained, but before she could exhale and calm down, a man sprang from the closet, wielding a silver dagger.

Allegra's breath caught as she met his deep, chocolate-brown gaze. His cold eyes lacked any emotion. His face bore heavy lines, yet an unmistakable strength and power emanated from him like a silent hum. He wore a heavy woolen coat and faded trousers cinched at the waist while four tarnished medals decorated his chest. None of the medals appeared familiar to Allegra. Clasped between his knotted fingers was a long knife, its blade glinting suspiciously in the dim light.

"Why are you here?" he demanded, his voice echoing off the walls.

"Shouldn't that be my question?" Allegra edged toward the door. Who was this man? He was old but not weak.

"Is the box there?" Dylan asked, halting abruptly upon seeing the man with the knife. "Who are you?"

"What's going on?" Esther crashed into Dylan's rear and jolted him forward. "*Oomph!*" She straightened. "Oh. How did you get inside? We locked the door."

The man's eyes flicked to Esther, and his grip tightened on the hilt. "I have come for the werewolf princess."

Allegra fought to keep an impassive expression. Had the council sent him? "I haven't the faintest idea what you're referring to."

His lips twisted into a cruel smile. "Don't lie to me, little princess. I know who you are and why the council wants you dead."

A cold sweat broke out on Allegra's forehead. She had always suspected her life was in danger, but hearing it confirmed terrified her. She searched the room for a weapon, but nothing was within reach.

Dylan stepped forward, his fists clenched. "You're not taking her anywhere."

The man laughed, a sound that sent shivers down Allegra's spine. "You think you can stop me, boy? I've been hunting werewolves longer than you've been alive."

Allegra's mind raced. She had to get out and protect herself and her friends. She stepped back, her gaze locked on the man's knife. With a roar, she launched herself at him, her claws extending from her fingertips.

He was fast, but Allegra was faster. She dodged his first strike and countered with a swipe of her claws, tearing through his coat and flesh. Blood splattered, and the man howled. Allegra lunged again, aiming for his throat, but he sidestepped and drove his knife deep into her side. She cried out, staggering back as pain consumed her.

Dylan shouted as he rushed to Allegra's aid. "Call Saber! Tell him we need him now, and it's urgent."

Allegra breathed through the agony radiating from the wound. She attempted to crawl backward and away from the old man. He stood, staring at her, his face expressionless while his medals swayed with each of his deep inhalations. Those medals and this man were peculiar.

He clearly knew her identity, but she couldn't think who he might be or how he'd discovered her.

"You were watching me last night." Her tongue felt weirdly thick while her side burned with the power of ten suns. "W-what d-did I tho to eew." No, that wasn't right. She opened her mouth to repeat her sentence, but her mind was quietly blank, the world foggy around the edges.

"Allegra!" Dylan shouted, his entire body tensing. A faint pleading note sounded in his voice. Something was severely wrong with her. While the wound would've hurt and blood dripped onto the floor, she was a wolf. She should've yanked the weapon free and continued fighting. This non-response alarmed him.

"What did you do to her?" he demanded.

"I coated the steel with a drug to subdue the wolf, and bleeding as she is, her human side won't last much longer."

The total unconcern in the old man raised Dylan's hackles. He cared, dammit. "Did you kill her parents and brother?" He'd keep him talking since he seemed disposed to chatter.

"My son took care of that mission," the man said without blinking.

"Your son?" Dylan repeated, disbelief in his voice.

A slow nod confirmed this. "He killed the royal family and received orders to take over the realm. They sent me to retrieve the princess and take her back to Val-des-Loups, dead or alive. And that's what I'll do."

Dylan's fists clenched. He refused to let the man seize Allegra. *His woman.* Dylan stumbled a fraction at the thought, then straightened his shoulders. It was nothing less than the truth. He had to stop the hunter and scanned for something to use as a weapon. He glanced at Allegra, and his heart sank. She lay still and limp, her eyes closed. She was unconscious, and he had no idea how to wake her.

The man sidled closer, another dagger appearing in his right hand.

Dylan had no choice. He lunged forward and tackled him, sending them both crashing to the floor.

Thumping footsteps sounded in the hall.

"Saber's here," Esther called.

"Stay back," Dylan shouted. "The knife blade contains poison. Yank it out of Allegra and press a pad against the wound. Call Gavin!"

The old man jabbed his elbow into Dylan's ribs, and Dylan gasped for breath. He was strong. So strong.

Esther ran to Allegra, seized her, and dragged her from the room.

The hunter stepped up a gear with renewed determination and fight. Dylan guessed he wanted to watch Allegra's demise so he could report back to the council.

The man feinted left but went right, the blade arcing outward and striking Dylan's biceps. Immediately, the skin turned numb, and blood poured from the wound.

"What's happening?" someone demanded.

Was that Saber? *Wow, whatever was on that blade was fast-acting.*

"Watch the knife," Dylan said, but his words didn't form properly and came out in gibberish.

A feminine voice interrupted, "Poison on the blade."

Dylan still grappled with the man, but he recognized Esther's voice. Suddenly, a roar echoed through the room, wild and familiar, causing the old man to release Dylan with an expression of terror.

A giant black cat stood in the doorway. Its eyes were green, and its fur shimmered under the light.

The man had no chance of escape, despite his scramble for freedom, because the cat lunged and darted low, ripping at the man's legs with his teeth. The hunter screamed, a shrill sound that echoed off the walls, then a gunshot sounded, and he toppled to the ground.

"Is he dead?" a feminine voice shouted.

"Dammit, Isabella. I wanted to interrogate him," Saber said. "We don't know who he is."

"I might recognize him," Isabella said. "I'm going around to the kitchen entrance. Don't shoot me."

Saber muttered something before turning to the big cat. "Thanks, Leo. He didn't cut you?"

The black leopard grunted and slipped out of the bedroom.

Dylan struggled to sit, and Saber helped him. "Is there anything in his pockets? Are we sure he's dead?"

Isabella entered the room and headed straight for the stranger. "What's with all the medals?"

"No idea," Saber said. "Dylan, stay with us. Gavin is on the way."

"Wash out the wound with cold water," Isabella suggested.

"Wait, I'm okay," Dylan said. "My wound is healing. I want to know if he's carrying identification."

"Whoa." Isabella whipped out her phone. "He's a shifter of some sort. Bird, I think, given his reaction to Leo." She snapped several photos. "His body is disintegrating. His face. This won't do much for your carpet. Hard to remove a stench like this."

Esther groaned. "Great. It would have to be my bedroom."

"How is Allegra?" Dylan asked as Saber helped him to stand.

"Gavin is here now," Esther called. "He thinks he knows what the poison is—something about the scent of it." She paused. "Allegra is coming around. Gavin has given her an antidote and says she'll be fine."

"Thank god," Dylan muttered, still feeling lightheaded. "The guy was so fast."

"We'll figure out who he is and why he wanted Allegra." Saber pulled out his phone. "We need to get a full description of him to the police."

"I'll take care of it," Isabella said.

Dylan reached for Allegra's hand, taking in the blood on her clothes and her bruised cheek. Her pale skin was almost translucent, and she winced as she tried to stand. At least she was alive. He had nearly lost her and hated the thought of something happening to her when he'd just found her. He made a quick decision.

Whatever the cost, he'd protect her.

Dylan helped her to bed, and once she'd settled and closed her eyes, he pulled out his phone to call Rory, his boss. No way in hell was she returning to Val-des-Loups without him.

EVERY PART OF HER body ached, even now. Hours later. Tired of lying in bed, she struggled into a dressing gown and trudged down the hall to the kitchen, where she'd heard Dylan and Esther talking in low voices.

Esther spotted her first. "What are you doing out of bed? Gavin told you to rest and give yourself time to heal."

"I'm fine. Just a little tired, and if I let myself snooze now, I won't sleep tonight. Have we learned anything more?"

"Isabella has," Dylan told her. "The man was a werewolf hunter, and his name was Leopold Adler. According to Isabella, Leopold has two sons. Johannes and Matthias have hundreds of kills between them. Isabella mentioned she has met Matthias and believes every word of his reputation."

"Oh. I thought werewolf killers were fictional." Her laugh sounded forced even to her. "Shows my inexperience."

"Dylan and I haven't heard of killers specific to werewolves, and we're wolves the same as you." Esther poured a mug of tea and shunted it toward Allegra. "I'll make you a sandwich. We're having dinner at the café if you're up to it."

Allegra felt the weight of Dylan's attention and turned his way. He was blaming himself.

"Stop," she ordered, subconsciously threading a note of steel in her voice. Once she realized this, she huffed out a breath. "Sorry. I must've absorbed more of my mother than I realized. But the sentiment is the same. This man—Leopold Adler—arrived in Middlemarch because of me. None of what has happened is your fault."

"But—"

"I mean it," Allegra said. "If anyone is to blame, it's me who brought trouble to Middlemarch. I've been thinking about what to do next, and it's clear that I need to head home immediately."

"But you'd decided to do that anyway," Esther said.

"That's true, but I didn't know about the werewolf hunters or the power the runes gave me over Val-des-Loups. I owe it to my people to rid the city and the kingdom of corruption. And that's my goal."

9

THE PRIVATE PLANE SOARED through the sky, nothing but blue ahead and puffy white clouds below. Isabella had pulled strings to make it possible, and their flight was much faster and smoother than Allegra's escape from the kingdom mere days ago. She studied the flashes of green forest, visible between the clouds, as the plane descended toward Val-des-Loups. Not long until they landed now.

Isabella's contact hadn't discovered anything more about Allegra's runes. However, Allegra was confident she'd learned enough to get by.

She stood, and when Dylan looked askance, she gestured at her baggy track pants and a casual T-shirt. "I'll do a quick change before we land. The council members are snobs and won't take me seriously in these clothes. According to Gabriel, appearances are everything."

Allegra had chosen her borrowed outfit with the utmost care, an ensemble of power and sophistication. The deep papaya suit fit her body like a glove, and she arranged her dark hair into a simple knot that complemented her blue eyes.

She tucked the runes into an inside jacket pocket. The black symbols fascinated and intrigued her, and a sense of peace and power filled her every time she was near them. Esther had made her a soft pouch to safely hold the symbols and prevent them from clacking together.

Right now, she recognized the strength from within, but doubt lingered in her mind. This was the moment when she either rose to the top or crumbled under pressure. Would she be able to make the council members answer her questions?

Yes!

This time, she would not skulk. She would demand information.

One or all of them was complicit in whatever was happening in her kingdom. They needed to cease treating her like a child because she was an adult and the only person capable of ruling if what her brother had written was true.

"Are you sure Leo and I won't stand out among the other residents and visitors?" Isabella asked.

Isabella and Leo had donned casual clothes. Dylan had dressed in smart casual, not wanting to detract from Allegra's more regal appearance. It was best if he faded into the background and let the council underestimate him. Let them think he was only after her money and position, a man seeking a good time and gleeful at his luck in meeting the princess.

As if.

Allegra knew the truth. They mightn't have known each other long, but she trusted him. That belief went a lot further than that she held for her council. She snorted and shook her head.

This plan would work because the council members were snobs. They saw what they wanted to see. So, she'd give them a show and make them think they'd won, or at least confuse them.

Leopold Adler's sons were a problem, but Isabella had feelers out to learn if they were still in the region or had moved on to their next job.

The plane landed and taxied before coming to a

halt. Isabella spoke briefly with the pilot before they exited and strode to the terminal. Dylan held the door open for her, a smile on his face and doing a slight bow. "Your Highness."

Allegra barely repressed the sensual shiver that tried to bolt through her and throw off her concentration. She'd miss him so much when he returned to Middlemarch. Allegra pushed that truth aside to focus. She swept through the doorway, spotted a man in a uniform behind a counter, and strode toward him.

"Princess Allegra," the man stuttered, "I thought you were sick, not expected to recover."

Allegra noted his name badge. He wore the official uniform of the border patrol agents but was young. She'd bet this post only had senior staff present when they expected an important visitor. Noticing the tense atmosphere and his shock, she asked, "Andrew, why would you assume that?"

"T-the council made an announcement two days ago. They stated that the royal physicians had been attending to you but were uncertain of the ailment, and we should prepare for bad news."

"Who gave the announcement?" Allegra asked,

keeping her smile gentle when she wanted to growl out her frustration. By leaving, she'd played right into their hands.

"Mr. Andersson and Mrs. Van der Meer. They appeared agitated. Everyone was upset, especially since your parents died—" He broke off abruptly, his face flushing.

"Was the entire council present during the announcement?" Allegra asked.

"Everyone was there except Ms. Rossi and Mr. Lindström," the young man said.

"Thank you," Allegra said. "Could you do me a favor, Andrew?"

"Anything, Princess Allegra." A faint pink tinged the tops of his ears.

Allegra smiled at him again. "Please don't tell anyone I'm here. I'm afraid something is wrong, and my friends and I need to fix this problem before it's too late. Could you do that for me?"

"Yes." Andrew straightened his shoulders and lifted his chin. "Anything else?"

Allegra arched a brow, silently communicating with Dylan, Isabella, and Leo.

Isabella stepped forward and handed Andrew a

business card. "If you don't hear on the news that Princess Allegra is better and is making changes, call this number and tell them everything."

Andrew swallowed. "H-how long should I wait?"

"Five days," Isabella said without hesitation.

"Five days," Andrew repeated, placing the card in his jacket pocket.

Allegra nodded. "Thank you, Andrew."

The quartet hailed a cab and proceeded to the chateau.

"Let's walk the rest of the way," Isabella suggested.

"Good idea. We should also check on the number of soldiers and any security measures that have changed during my absence," Allegra said.

Allegra led the other three along cobblestone streets and narrow lanes, past shops with bay windows and vendors selling their wares directly from carts. A man pushing a cart trundled toward them, a smile wreathing his grizzled, wrinkled face, but no recognition lit his eyes.

Shame filled Allegra. Many of her subjects didn't recognize her because she'd been away at school for years. Once she'd arrived home for good, she'd lingered around the chateau, mourning the loss of her family. Her indecision and lack of action had allowed the council to take over.

That would change.

At the corner of a block of shops and a small group of traders with outdoor stalls, Allegra studied the main chateau gate.

"More guards than usual," Allegra murmured when the others joined her.

"We want to avoid security," Isabella said. "Is there another way into the grounds?"

"Yes, but circling the walls and city will take us half an hour. I use my private exit when I go running alone. Pierre showed it to me when I was home one time, and we went out together." Allegra squeezed her eyes closed for an instant and shoved aside the wave of grief. The old werewolf hunter hadn't cared that his sons had killed her family, but the financial reward had excited him. The blood money.

"This way." Allegra waited for a guard to alter his path before dashing around the corner and into an alley. At least she knew her way around her city. Eventually, she'd become familiar with her people.

She strode forward, her sensitive nose picking up a cacophony of distinct scents. The fragrant aroma of fresh food, the earthy bouquet of ripe vegetables, and the sweet fragrance of blooming flowers filled her nostrils, bringing a faint smile.

But as she ventured deeper into the less-known parts of the city, the pleasant smells gave way to less savory ones. The tang of motor oil mixed with a faint body odor, creating an overpowering stench that made her wrinkle her nose in distaste. Laundry strung across the lane dripped on their heads while the entire place reeked of decay. Pierre had brought her here, but the contamination hadn't been this bad.

"A poorer part of the city," Dylan said, keeping step with her.

"Yes." The council should've helped the residents in this area.

As she passed a nearby warehouse, another miasma reached her sensitive nose. The sickly-sweet odor of rotting refuse mingled with the mold, creating a potent combination that made her stomach churn.

Her subjects required help, and she intended to see they received it.

Gradually, the squalor of the properties compressed in the city's center lay behind them, and a cleaner, fresher herbal fragrance rode in the air.

"The next section runs close to a guard station, so no talking, and watch where you step," Allegra whispered.

She led them past the thick stone wall while listening to the laughter of the off-duty guards. A meaty scent filled her breath, along with the yeasty goodness of freshly baked bread. She checked her watch and saw more time had passed than she'd realized.

The forest lay ahead, and the whisper of the wind in the leaves and the sweet, nutty, almost buttery scent of the oaks made it seem like she was home.

A faint rustle, immediately followed by the sharp tingle against her chest, slowed her steps. Behind her, Dylan, Leo, and Isabella halted.

Allegra's senses sharpened as she cautiously approached the bushes, foreboding creeping up her spine. She could feel the weight of the runes, their magical energy pulsing against her skin. Allegra's muscles tensed, and she slowly reached for the hilt of the werewolf hunter's silver dagger at her waist. She inhaled, attempting to calm her nerves. Behind her, her friends pulled out weapons, their senses informing them of the same danger she perceived.

As she inched closer, Allegra saw a rustling in the bushes, and her heart rate spiked. She froze when the branches shifted, revealing something moving within. Allegra's fingers tightened around the dagger's hilt as she prepared for the worst.

She took a step back, positioning herself for a better vantage point. Her gaze darted left and right, trying to assess any potential threats.

Without warning, a tall and lean blond with wild blue eyes sprang at her. A snarl highlighted his sharp and angular features. A second man with a more rugged and muscular build charged her like an enraged bull.

The runes vibrated painfully against her chest, and she flinched, her body jerking to the right and away from the sudden torment. Seconds later, a knife whistled past her face.

"Stop, or I'll shoot," Dylan ordered.

"What happened to our father?" the muscular man thundered. His gray eyes flashed with rage.

"Ah, the werewolf hunter's sons," Isabella said.

"She killed him," the man with the blue eyes accused Allegra.

"No, she didn't, but if she had, it would've been

self-defense," Isabella said.

Allegra's body remained coiled, ready to spring into action. "You killed my mother and father. My brother," she said, her tone flat.

The blond shrugged while his brown-haired brother released a snigger.

"What of it?" the brown-haired one said. "The best way to deal with a werewolf is to slay it."

"Why?" Dylan demanded before she could.

"A wolf killed our mother and sister and left our aunt and uncle badly injured. They lasted just a day before they succumbed to their wounds."

"My parents didn't do it," Allegra snapped.

"The only good werewolf is a dead one," the brown-haired man shouted and charged, jabbing his knife with lightning speed. Allegra blinked as a shot rang out, causing the man to stumble.

"Blast it, Matthias," the blond shouted. He pulled a weapon from his belt, but another round resounded before he could clear his firearm. He cursed and squeezed off a shot, but it went wide.

Allegra sprang at the blond, taking him unawares. He fell back but lashed out, catching her in the thigh.

"Dylan," Isabella snapped, her gun in hand.

"Got him," Dylan said.

"You all right, Allegra?" Leo asked, helping her up.

"Fine." Not exactly the truth, but the runes had warned her, driving her to shift direction. Although the blond had kicked her, the injury wasn't as bad as it might've been. She picked herself up, the flash of something green attracting her attention. "That's Pierre's ring. It went missing from his chamber on the morning of the walkabout."

Brown hair sniggered, unconcerned. "The one where I shot him."

"They're shifters, too," Isabella said in a harsh voice. "Birds. Watch them closely."

"Aren't you the clever one?" Blondie's nostrils flared.

"Wolves and a feline. Guess you lose." He flicked a knife at Leo, the green of the stone flashing in the ring he wore.

Leo didn't move quite fast enough, the blade striking his forearm. He cursed, and Isabella calmly fired at Blondie. When Brown Hair spun toward her to help his brother, Isabella shot him too. Seconds later, she sprang at him, kneeing him in the back and effortlessly clipping on a pair of handcuffs that Allegra hadn't noticed earlier.

"Leo, you okay?" Isabella asked.

"I'm fine," he said, sounding a touch grouchy. "Get the other guy."

Allegra stalked toward Blondie. He wasn't moving, but she wouldn't assume he was dead until she confirmed it. Allegra shoved the man onto his back, then crouched beside him.

Isabella had shot him in the head, the hole in his forehead a clue as to his health. She removed Pierre's ring and rolled to her feet. "Dead."

"What will we do with him?" Leo asked, gesturing at the other man.

"Let's gag and stash him in the trees until later."

"No!" the man protested. He hadn't responded to his brother's death, which was strange given his earlier reaction to his father.

Isabella gagged him and dragged him behind a bush. She reappeared several minutes later. "He's tired and is napping while we're away."

A snort escaped from Leo.

Allegra tucked the ring in the same pocket that held the runes and, weirdly, the heat and energy emanating from the pouch increased. It swept through her chest in a tingling surge of vigor. *Wow.* She rocked on her feet, grabbing for mental balance.

"What's wrong?" Dylan asked.

"Let's go." Allegra led the way to the gate she used to exit the chateau grounds secretly. That was interesting. She wanted to contemplate the talisman and the symbols before she discussed them with anyone. Somehow, the ring increased the rune's strength. She felt more robust and in control. Connected to the land. She felt powerful.

"We need to treat everyone we meet as suspicious," Isabella warned in an undertone. "We can't trust anyone."

"It might make sense for us to split up. Less chance of someone spotting us."

"I'm not intending to skulk." Allegra checked her watch. "The council will be finishing the weekly meeting and about to start on the food and drink. I intend to confront them and demand answers."

"Not so great if one of them shoots you," Isabella said.

"We should stay together." Dylan reached for Allegra's hand. He squeezed it, and everything in her melted. Their relationship had happened fast but having him at her side seemed right.

Allegra's heart pounded fiercely as though it might burst out of her chest. Her breaths came in quick, shallow gasps, betraying the sheer magnitude of the emotions raging inside her. Intense energy emanated from her breastbone, where the runes and ring rested.

"My gut tells me I need to hustle and confront them." Her words were a mere whisper compared to the thundering beat of her pulse. But it was an understatement, a paltry description of the fierce urgency that consumed her. Every fiber of her being cried out for action, for resolution, for justice.

10

ALLEGRA LED THEM THROUGH the chateau, past the gaping servants and a sole guard who appeared perplexed by their sudden appearance. She marched up the spiral staircase, her footsteps ringing in the enclosed space. At the top of the stairs, she turned toward the Octagon Room. When they arrived, the large oak door was closed, but her wolfish hearing caught the shouts coming from within the chamber. She inched the door open with care, holding her breath and releasing it when the hinges didn't creak.

The Octagon was a large, circular room with eight sides, each representing a unique part of the kingdom. Tapestries and majestic portraits of past rulers lined the walls, and mid-room, the large table was the hub of activity. Currently, the six council members argued loudly about Allegra.

"Where is Allegra?" Maria Rossi demanded. "I know this illness is a fabrication. Where is she now?

"Rubbish," Gabriel Andersson said. "She is in her room, and the doctors wish to keep her isolated if she has caught the virus circulating in Europe. A pandemic is the last thing we want."

"I don't understand any of this," Andreas Lindström said. "Allegra is right. All is not right in the kingdom. She was right to call us out."

"That has nothing to do with Allegra's illness," Sophia van der Meer stated.

Yeah, Allegra just bet it didn't. Impulse had her removing the ring from the pouch and sliding it onto her right hand's middle finger. At first, the golden band holding the emerald stone was too large, but it pulled tight until it fit her finger snugly and was in no danger of slipping off.

With the runes sending out pulses of confidence and power, Allegra boldly stepped into the room. She cleared her throat, causing the conversation to cease abruptly. All eyes turned toward her as she stood before them, her friends flanking her on either side.

"I'm here for answers," she said calmly but firmly.

"Werewolf hunters killed my parents and brother. While I was with my friends in Middlemarch, a hunter tried to kill me. I believe one of you organized the hit."

"Us?" Maria asked, her eyebrows rising and her tone disbelieving.

The council members exchanged uneasy glances, and tension rose in the room. This confrontation could turn ugly, but she was determined to get answers.

"Princess Allegra," Gabriel Andersson said, his voice thick with patently false concern. "We're so glad to see you're feeling better. We were discussing the best way to handle this situation."

"What situation?" Allegra asked, her eyes narrowing.

"You're the last surviving royal in our kingdom. If you're not well, we need to make alternative arrangements," Sophia van der Meer said. "Someone to step into your shoes. You're so young and inexperienced."

"And you want to take over. I am the ruling royal, and that won't change," she said, with a snap in her voice as she observed each council member's reaction. "This pushing me around will cease. Doing your own thing without seeking my permission will halt. I am the princess, and this is my realm. *Mine.* You assist me. Nothing more."

One or two of the council seemed genuinely perplexed, while the rest displayed various stages of anger. A blood vessel pulsed at Gabriel's temple, and his face turned red. Allegra stared him down when she would've acted with diffidence in the past. The runes tingled, and the emerald ring glowed. It was subtle, but she noticed because of the heat accompanying the radiance.

"I don't know what you're talking about," Sophia said, snooty expression back in place. "You're feverish and rambling."

"You've lied to me," Allegra snapped. "And spread rumors about my health and whereabouts to the kingdom, causing unnecessary fear and panic. One or more of you colluded and arranged werewolf hunters to kill the rest of my family—"

"We would never," Maria said, her rapid blinking and pale cheeks showing shock.

"You used my absence to undermine and prepare for a coup. You thought you could easily take over my kingdom by getting rid of me."

The room fell silent as Allegra's words hung in the air. The council members shifted uncomfortably in their seats, unsure how to respond to the accusations.

"Princess Allegra, you're paranoid." Gabriel tried to regain control of the situation. "We simply wanted to ensure the kingdom's stability in unforeseen circumstances."

Allegra laughed bitterly. "Unforeseen circumstances? You mean my sudden disappearance and the subsequent rumors about my illness? Arranging my parents' assassination. My brother's assassination. Paying someone to shoot at me when I was running in the forest."

Indignant objections broke out.

"Enough!" She slashed her hand through the air. "I am the princess, and it is my right to rule Val-des-Loups. It is tradition."

Gabriel's mouth twisted into a sneer. "You're a child. You're not capable of ruling this kingdom."

"Who are they?" Sophia asked belatedly. "This is a private meeting room. Call the guards and get rid of them."

"We're Princess Allegra's private security," Isabella said in a stern, take-no-prisoner tone.

Sophia sniffed. "What is wrong with the chateau guards?"

"We can't trust them," Allegra said, her gaze still fixed on Gabriel. "I don't trust them."

"Your paranoia is getting the better of you," Gabriel spat, his eyes flashing with temper. The growl of his wolf bled into his voice, making it guttural. "I do not have ulterior motives and don't want to start a coup. We only want what's best for Val-des-Loups."

Allegra stood her ground. "What's beneficial for Val-des-Loups is for me to take my rightful position as the monarch," she declared. "And for you to answer for your crimes."

Gabriel's control frayed at Allegra's words. His gaze darted around the room, his breath coming in short, ragged gasps. It appeared he might lash out for a moment, but then he regained his composure, his features smoothing into a mask of calm.

"You have no proof," he said. "These are baseless accusations fueled by your insecurities and paranoia."

But he didn't fool Allegra. She could see the guilt lurking behind Gabriel's eyes, the flicker of fear that betrayed his true nature.

"You're lying," she snapped. "I know what you've

done. You're responsible for the bad things that have happened in Val-des-Loups, the misfortune our people have suffered."

Gabriel's expression twisted into a sneer. "And what do you plan to do about it?" he spat. "Once again. You're just a child and have no power, no authority. You're nothing."

Ah! But she had the runes and had noticed an interesting detail upon entering the room. All eight walls featured a glyph in the center of the illustration, each equal in size to the ones in her possession.

Allegra met Gabriel's gaze before shifting to Sophia. The woman sneered at her, but Allegra didn't react. She stood tall, her chin held high and spoke with the strength and conviction of a genuine leader. "I am Princess Allegra." Her voice rang out in a clear, commanding tone. "And I will do whatever it takes to protect my kingdom and its people. Even if that means taking down a traitor like you."

Without warning, Gabriel's control snapped. He released a guttural snarl, his eyes blazing with feral rage. Instantly, he was on his feet, his body contorting as he transformed into his wolf.

The room erupted into shouts and threats. Sophia,

Maximilian, and Emilio morphed into wolves and lunged at Allegra. But she was ready. As were Dylan, Isabella, and Leo.

Allegra leaped into action with a fierce battle cry, the silver dagger flashing in the air as she fought to protect her kingdom. A thunderous shot rang out, and Maximilian went down.

"Don't kill anyone," Allegra shouted. "Take them alive."

Isabella and Leo took care of Emilio and Maximilian with ease, leaving them zip-tied and helpless. It became clear that Maria and Andreas were on their side, since they stood, their hands raised and horror on their features.

Sophia darted forward and backhanded Allegra across the nose, striking her hard enough to make her head ring. She gasped, blood trickling down her chin. Every muscle in Allegra tightened upon seeing the savage joy on Sophia's face.

"Come on, runes. Help me here." Immediately, power surged through her, and she staggered into Sophia's swing, taking the woman by surprise.

Allegra balled her fist and punched Sophia, knocking the councilor on her arse. Isabella grabbed her, and before Sophia knew what had happened, Isabella and Leo had her secured with zip-ties. Allegra hoped they were strong enough to contain a werewolf.

She joined Dylan, taking pleasure in subtlety, herding Gabriel into a corner. Gabriel bared his teeth, but high living had made him lazy. He'd gained weight and hadn't kept up his fitness. Right now, his sides heaved. Allegra had the upper hand, and he knew it. He snarled, his hackles visibly rising. Allegra and Dylan exchanged glances and communicated without words. They rushed him, and although he tried, he was too unfit to keep fighting.

"Shift," Allegra demanded.

Gabriel glared at her. Allegra grasped a handful of his black fur. She shook him, and a green shimmer sparkled from the band on her finger. An instant later, Gabriel shifted.

"How did you do that?" he demanded, his sides heaving. "I've heard rumors, but I thought a forced shift was a myth and the stuff of legends.

"The runes speak to me," Allegra said, and she suspected the ring since it still glowed. "They guide my actions and give me the power to rule the kingdom."

Gabriel made a scoffing sound. "Old wives' tales."

"Think what you want. I don't care." Allegra turned to Maria and Andreas. "Is there someone we can trust from the palace guards?"

Andreas tugged on his gray vest, straightening his garments. Spots of blood had sprayed on his cheeks, and his ruffled hair spoiled his typical immaculate appearance. "Yes, of course. I will summon them immediately."

Dylan ran his fingers down her cheek. "Are you okay?" His hazel eyes were full of sympathy.

Her heart gave a tiny wrench because she liked this man so much. She would stay here to fix her kingdom and find trustworthy wolves to replace the traitors on the council. He would travel home. She pushed her wave of melancholy away and scanned the chamber. "I noticed that each of the eight walls holds a rune. It occurred to me the symbols are of a similar size to the ones I have. Do you think those have always been here?"

"You think they're fakes?"

"Yeah." The glyphs buzzed against her chest, almost like a signal of approval.

"Only one way to find out." Dylan approached the

nearest one, knife in hand.

"You can't remove those," Maria said in horror. "They give the ruler and the council the ability to rule. I doubt you'll be able to remove them. Long ago, a thief broke into the chamber. He tried to remove a rune. It zapped him. My grandmother told me he was comatose for three days before he recovered."

"Except they haven't been working lately," Allegra said. "Go ahead, Dylan. Wait, do you want me to do it?"

Dylan passed his fingers over the rune and gingerly touched it. "I don't feel anything wrong. There's no current or weird sensation." He applied the tip of the knife and seconds later held the glyph in his hand. "It slid out easily."

"What?" Maria said. "That doesn't seem right."

"It looks like the runes you have, but the weight differs." Dylan handed it to her.

She felt nothing, and Dylan was right. It was much lighter than those in her possession. A soft current ran down her arm without warning and settled in her palm. The fake rune shifted from black to a fiery red that seared her eyeballs with its brightness. She closed her eyes, and when she opened her fingers again, nothing remained but ash. She gaped at her hand, but there was no soreness. No wound. Instead, an insistent buzz emanated from her jacket pocket. She pressed her fingers to her breastbone. "Okay. I get it," she muttered. "Hold your horses."

Dylan grinned. "Talking to yourself is a sign of madness."

"Remove the other runes from the wall," she said. "Please."

"My pleasure."

"Don't let her do that," Gabriel ordered. "Stop her."

Allegra cocked her head, surveying the room and the council members. "When I was a child, this room shimmered with a soft green. I'd forgotten that until I saw the ring's glow."

Gabriel scowled. "Those bastards took the ring instead of giving it to me."

"The jewel is only part of the spell," Allegra said, taking out the runes. The first and second glyphs remained onyx, but the third radiated a soft green. Walking over to the wall, she pressed the green rune against the spot where the false one had sat. The rune glowed a deeper green before returning to its original color. Allegra could've sworn the building sighed. She glanced over her shoulder and saw from the others' reaction that it hadn't been her imagination.

"Replace the other runes," Dylan said. "I think they've been waiting to come home."

"I don't understand. Why did Pierre give the runes to me with no explanation?" Allegra whispered to Dylan.

"Did something happen around the same time?" Dylan asked. "Something that might've changed the course of tradition?"

Allegra placed the second rune in its correct position, and this time a soft blue glowed. She replaced the other runes individually until she'd returned all eight to their original positions.

"Did anything happen when I was sixteen?" Allegra asked Maria.

Gabriel snarled, and the room pulsated with color. Andreas returned with four palace guards, and the colors vanished when they entered the room.

"Take them to the dungeon and hold them until we formally charge them," Allegra said.

"Leo and I will go with them. You don't need us, right?" Isabella asked.

"No. Thank you." Allegra turned her focus back to the remaining council.

"Maria? Andreas? What happened when I was sixteen? I wasn't here because my parents sent me to boarding school. I seldom returned home. Pierre gave me these runes and told me to hide them and not to tell anyone."

Maria and Andreas exchanged a glance before Maria spoke. "There were rumors that your father had an affair, and a child resulted."

Dylan edged closer to Allegra, and she welcomed his silent support. She tried to think back, but her parents had always been distant. She'd thought their lack of attention was because of their busy schedules.

"Was it true?" she asked.

"Not exactly. The king's younger brother had an affair, and you were that child," Maria said. "The king's brother and his lover were murdered, but with his dying breath, your father asked the king to raise you."

"Who knew about this?" Allegra asked, trying to make sense of everything.

"Few," Andreas said. "Gabriel told us when he informed us we couldn't let you take over as the ruler because you weren't of royal blood."

"But it sounds as if I was a baby when I came to the chateau," Allegra said. "What changed?"

Maria snapped her fingers. "That might've been when someone tried to shoot Pierre. Your father, or rather your uncle, had continual clashes with him. They disagreed on the direction the kingdom should take to secure the future. The king wanted Pierre to marry. Pierre refused because he didn't like the candidates, and there was the failed assassination attempt."

"You're implying my brother didn't trust his father," Allegra said.

Andreas nodded. "That was the impression I received."

"Well, I'm here and have restored the runes to their rightful place."

A burst of color greeted her words, a sense of approval wafting through the chamber.

"You're also wearing the ruler's ring," Maria said with a smile.

Andreas nodded. "You will be good for the kingdom."

"Why didn't you stop Gabriel and the others?"

Dylan asked.

"Two against four. We could only support the princess and vote against the rest of the council. When you disappeared, we feared the worst," Andreas said. "We're glad you're back. We will support you as always."

Allegra inclined her head. "Thank you."

"Can we do anything else to help?" Maria asked.

"We will meet here tomorrow," Allegra said. "It's time to plan for Val-des-Loups' future."

"We are at your disposal." Andreas bowed while Maria dipped in a curtsy. They left, leaving her alone with Dylan.

"You are amazing," Dylan said.

The room glowed for an instant as if agreeing, and he grinned.

Allegra sighed and closed the distance between them. She wrapped her arms around his neck and kissed him, putting every one of her emotions and feelings into the kiss. When their lips finally parted, he sent her a quizzical look.

"What's wrong?" he asked.

"I'll miss you when you go home," she said, a physical ache in her chest at the thought of parting.

He cocked his head. "Who mentioned going home? I thought I'd stick around and make myself useful. I talked to my boss, Rory, before we left and told him how I felt about you. He informed me I'd be a fool to let you go, and he'd ended up in Middlemarch because he'd followed his heart and Anita. I agreed with his assessment."

Allegra blinked as a slow grin spread across his face. "You're staying? But what about Esther? Your home? I thought you had commitments."

"Allegra." He brushed the hair away from her face. "You're here, and you've become important to me. Esther will understand. I want to be with you, and we can visit Middlemarch as often as we want. I hope to share your bed and love you—if you're agreeable."

"Yes!" she shrieked, happiness filling her. "Yes, I'd like that very much."

"Thank goodness for that." Dylan winked at her. "Let's seal our agreement with a kiss." He dipped his head and kissed her long and deep, and the chamber pulsed in a storm of vivid color while the princess embraced her man.

THANK YOU FOR READING My Valiant Princess. I hope you enjoyed reading about Allegra and Dylan's romance. We're back to the gathering proper in the next book, **My Highland Wedding**. This is Edwina's story, and she's a little irritated when a handsome stranger manhandles her and carries her out of the ballroom.

Learn more about My Highland Wedding today! (www.shelleymunro.com/books/my-highland-wedding)

ABOUT AUTHOR

USA Today bestselling author Shelley Munro lives in Auckland, the City of Sails, with her husband and a cheeky Jack Russell/mystery breed dog.

Typical New Zealanders, Shelley and her husband left home for their big OE soon after they married (translation of New Zealand speak - big overseas experience). A twelve-month-long adventure lengthened to six years of roaming the world. Enduring memories include being almost sat on by a mountain gorilla in Rwanda, lazing on white sandy beaches in India, whale watching in Alaska, searching for leprechauns in Ireland, and dealing with ghosts in an English pub.

While travel is still a big attraction, these days Shelley is most likely found in front of her computer following another love - that of writing stories of contemporary and paranormal romance and adventure. Other interests include watching rugby (strictly for research purposes), cycling, playing croquet and the ukelele, and curling up with an enjoyable book.

Visit Shelley at her Website

www.shelleymunro.com

Join Shelley's Newsletter

www.shelleymunro.com/newsletter

ALSO BY SHELLEY

Paranormal

Middlemarch Shifters
My Scarlet Woman
My Younger Lover
My Peeping Tom
My Assassin
My Estranged Lover
My Feline Protector
My Determined Suitor
My Cat Burglar
My Stray Cat
My Second Chance
My Plan B
My Cat Nap

My Romantic Tangle
My Blue Lady
My Twin Trouble
My Precious Gift

Middlemarch Gathering
My Highland Mate
My Highland Fling
My Elusive Mate
My Valiant Princess
My Highland Wedding

Middlemarch Capture
Snared by Saber
Favored by Felix
Lost with Leo
Spellbound with Sly
Journey with Joe
Star-Crossed with Scarlett

www.ingramcontent.com/pod-product-compliance
Lightning Source LLC
Chambersburg PA
CBHW051952170626
46808CB00007B/2578